D1579404

## About the Author

Jane Burns retired from teaching English in 2009 to concentrate on writing. In 2013, she completed a Masters Degree in Television Fiction Writing which led to a stint as Educational Consultant on popular BBC 1 school drama Waterloo Road. *My Sister's My Teacher!* is Jane's first attempt at a children's novel.

## Dedication

To…John Burns – My youngest brother who was a pupil
in my English class during his first year of high school
and my very first teaching post.

Jane Burns

# My Sister's My Teacher!

AUSTIN MACAULEY
PUBLISHERS LTD.

A CIP catalogue record for this title is available from the British Library.

ISBN 9781786124821 (Paperback)
ISBN 9781786124838 (Hardback)
ISBN 9781786124845 (E-Book)

www.austinmacauley.com

First Published (2017)
Austin Macauley Publishers Ltd.
25 Canada Square
Canary Wharf
London
E14 5LQ

# Introduction

# A Potted History of Coatbridge and Summerlee

What can I say about my home town, Coatbridge? It doesn't boast an ancient castle; there were no famous battles fought here; no famous lifesaving inventions were ever developed here; no famous explorers have left its streets to discover new worlds.

It did, however, once boast a canal – the Monklands Canal – which was a busy thoroughfare at the height of the Industrial Revolution. If your teacher hasn't touched upon that part of Scottish History because you were too busy finding out how the Pyramids were built in Egypt, it's enough for you to know that once upon a time, Coatbridge was a hive of industry. My Grandfather and my Great-grandfather worked in its engineering firms, travelled on its trams and were saddened when modernisation left these proud industries behind. Their town once boasted *three* separate cinemas and a proper theatre.

Today, *my* home town boasts one shopping centre, no cinemas or theatres. The canal has been filled in, and the only remnant of the Industrial Revolution is to be found in its one tourist attraction – The Summerlee Heritage Park – which is just across the road from my home and is overlooked by my local school, Summerlee Primary (which is where most of this story takes place).

Summerlee Primary is an old, red brick building, perched at the top of Academy Street. It's the oldest primary school in Coatbridge now. I've always been fascinated by the building, imagining all of the different boys and girls who have trudged in and out of its huge, heavy doors, for a period of over a hundred years. But, this is its last year before a new high-tech building opens and we are the final Primary Seven intake who will pass through its doors ...

# Chapter 1

## Surprise, Surprise...

I should have known my final year at Summerlee Primary School would be a disaster by the weather. The morning started off with grey clouds which had turned to purple by the time my best friend Holly, and I arrived at the school gates.

The middle of August, but it was more like the middle of winter in Summerlee!

And to think that only two weeks ago, I had been sunning myself on the top deck of the Island Escape, in the middle of the Mediterranean, with nothing to worry me but whether or not I had used sufficient dollops of sun block or whether my freckles were too *freckly*. I was dying to show off my holiday pics to my pals. The photos were still on my mobile because Dad hadn't been around to upload them onto the computer and print them out on to proper photo paper.

I so wanted to boast about the fabulous places we had visited – Minorca, Rome, Pompeii and Cannes. I would have plenty to write about this year. Teachers always get you to write about your Summer Holiday that first day back. This year I wouldn't mind at all. I had enough postcards and souvenirs to do History Projects, Geography Projects, and Anything-at-all-to-do-with-holidays Projects. I could be the Project Queen this year – if only our school had such an award.

Holly and I met up with identical twins, Debbie and Louise Randall, who were their usual pristine selves, with their matching white shirts, identical ties tied in identical knots, and navy blue pleated pinafores. Their chestnut brown ponytails were tied back with blue and navy voile ribbons. They had even acquired matching braces on their top teeth. (Rob, who is going to marry my sister and become my brother-in-law, is their dentist. His Dental Surgery is just down the street from our school. The surgery is on the bottom floor of a detached sandstone house and Rob has a flat above. That's where my big sister, Angela, will go to live once they are married.)

"Oh," they sighed in unison, "we would *love* to go on a cruise. Imagine visiting France, Spain and Italy all during *one* holiday!" They took my mobile and flicked through the photos, commenting with more sighs and *ooohs* and *aaahs* that each picture was more fabulous than the previous one.

"I can't wait to see the actual photos, Sam," said Debbie as she handed back the phone to me.

"We didn't go abroad this year," added Louise. "Mum said we couldn't afford it because of the new conservatory we had put in during the Easter Break."

"We did spend a lovely week in a caravan at St. Andrews though, at the beginning of July. Remember?" said Debbie.

"Oh, yes, it was great," said Louise smiling at the memory, "but it all seems so long ago now."

"Well, you three are lucky to get away at all," said Holly, but without a hint of envy. "My parents said that because of the *Credit Crunch*, we were cutting back on holidays this year. So, when it comes to summer holiday stories, Sam, I'll just have to borrow yours."

14

We all laughed heartily when Holly suggested hiring out my various holiday experiences for the price of a packet of cheese and onion crisps and a can of Irn-Bru (per person, of course).

Holly could be quite funny at times. Nothing seemed to get her down. Her dad has his own roofing business which has been going through a sticky patch. Her mum is a Staff Nurse at the local hospital, so at least they still have a regular wage coming in. These days, so it seemed to us, people were either losing businesses or being made redundant – like my dad was from his job at the bank. We didn't really understand the *Credit Crunch* which everyone was talking about and which took up most of the time in news bulletins.

But children tend to worry about things which only affect them and we were no different, I suppose. The important questions which occupied our thinking were: Would Bully Bella be back to annoy us for another year? Would *Ms. Snobby*, (that's our nickname for Ms. Snodgrass, the snooty but strict Principal Teacher) have many red blotches which she would be desperate to cover up with smart trouser suits? And the most important matter for us: *who would Mr Bamber, the Head Teacher, get to replace our beloved Mrs McNulty as our teacher?*

Mrs McNulty had been our teacher forever before she decided to retire to look after her grandchildren. You would think she had seen enough children in her teaching career without carrying on into her retirement!

The bell rang to summon us to our first Assembly of the new school session, and our last year of primary education. Holly, the Twins and I made our way into the building, laughing and chatting and saying 'Hi' to as many people as possible while we crushed our way into the Assembly Hall which doubled as a gym during term time.

Because we were now the Senior Pupils, we were at the very back of the hall, which made it difficult to see the whole of the stage, and which teachers were already seated behind Mr Bamber. The buzz of excited chatter gradually melted away when Mr Bamber came forward and adjusted the wobbly microphone. He cleared his throat, blinked a few times for good measure, smiled down at us and began his by now (to us P7 pupils anyway) familiar *Welcome Back To Summerlee Primary Speech.*

"Boys and Girls, from Primary Two right up to Primary Seven, a very big welcome back to Summerlee Primary! You are all looking very fresh, some of you very suntanned, and certainly very well turned out by your parents and guardians for this next exciting stage of your young careers."

Holly leaned over and whispered to me, "I bet he sniffs the air round about now." And sure enough, he looked up at the ceiling and did that snorting, sniffing thing he does, as though there is a bad smell in the air and he's trying to work out what it is. (My dad says he's probably nervous when it comes to public speaking. He says he saw a lot of men like that in the banking world.) How could such an important man like the Head of a whole school be nervous about talking to children? I could maybe understand it if he was addressing Miss Prim (the most ancient teacher in the school, if not the world) or *Ms. Snobby*, but *us*?

I was so lost in these thoughts that I missed the next part of his speech. Holly was frantically tugging at my blazer sleeve (Primary Seven pupils have to wear blazers, shirts and ties instead of the customary polo shirts with the school logo – to make us feel more grown up, and make the younger pupils look up to us, so we were told by Mrs McNulty before she abandoned us to our fate). Holly was still shaking the life out of me and pointing to the stage. I had missed Mr Bamber introducing our new teacher. I stood up, straining forward eagerly to catch a glimpse – only to find out why Holly was so frantic.

There on the stage beside Mr Bamber stood MY BIG SISTER ANGELA!

"...and I am sure our Primary Seven boys and girls will benefit from the excellent skills which our newest teacher, Miss Winters, will bring to the school. As a former pupil and Head Girl herself, she knows the importance of education and doing one's best. In fact, she is a prime example of what Education can do for *you...*"

Mr Bamber prattled on with Our Angela smiling up at him, looking out eagerly towards the back of the Hall where we were seated. I felt myself being pulled back into my chair by Holly. There were hushed voices and sniggering as people in our class realised that our new, young and inexperienced teacher was actually *my sister*. I wanted the floor to open up and swallow me. Everything around me was a blur. It was like being in one of those nightmares where you couldn't find your way home, no matter how you tried.

"You kept that quiet, Sam," hissed Holly in my right ear.

"I hadn't the foggiest she was coming to our school. I didn't even know she had any kind of job, let alone one in our school!"

"Imagine your Angela being our new teacher!" exclaimed the Twins at once in my left ear. "Will you have to call her Miss Winters instead of Angela?"

Fortunately, we were being ushered out of the hall to our classrooms, so I didn't have to tell the Twins all of the things I would be calling Our Angela when I got home.

I was suddenly very popular as we made our way noisily along the corridor to Room 10, our new classroom. It's the first time I have known Paul Rankin and Andrew Roberts to talk about anything other than football.

"Your Angela's going to be our teacher, then," said Paul, "so does that mean you'll get off with doing homework then?"

"If that's the case, Sam, can you get us off it too?" asked Andrew.

Trust boys to think of an angle. I had worse things to worry about. How was I going to live down the embarrassment? I'd heard of pupils being at the same schools where their parents were teachers, but never being *taught* by a sister who was *only* ten years older! I had made up my mind about one thing – even before we got inside Room 10: There wasn't room for the two of us in this school let alone this classroom!

# Chapter 2

## Every Picture Tells a Story

As you can imagine, the rest of the day couldn't pass quickly enough for me. Angela got down to the business of being a teacher straight away. She quickly took the register, calling out my name as *Samantha* Winters, sending the class into a fit of snorts from the boys and giggles from the girls. Bully Bella Hendry muttered loud enough for the whole class to hear, "Huh! Some teacher she's going to be! She doesn't even know her own sister's name. Either that or she's just trying to be posh."

Nobody really laughed at that except Bella and her new cronies Jade Jones and Danielle Doyle, who were now in the same group. At least, Angela hadn't put Bella in *my* group. I was thankfully beside Holly and the Twins again, but Andrew and Paul were in a different group.

It was weird to see my own sister giving out commands and everyone obeying her. I think the boys thought she was some kind of goddess, so they were falling over themselves to become Milk Monitors, Tuck Shop Monitors or Tray Monitors *or* be given any kind of duty where they would have to seek her advice or approval. The girls, (all except for me and Bella), asked her lots of questions about her clothes and jewellery. Now, Our Angela has always had style, and I knew she would give *Ms. Snobby* serious competition in the clothes department – if you get my meaning. At any other time I would have been pleased to see the looks of admiration – but not today.

Why couldn't she be in somebody else's school and then she could be admired till the cows come home?

During the lunch break, Holly, the Twins and I went to the Cafeteria. Mrs Crangle – or Betty, as she liked to be called – made my day even more miserable by announcing that she was now running an 'Eco Cafe', because this year, one of the School's aims was to become an ECO SCHOOL.

"Couldn't you have waited till next year, Betty, after we have gone?" I moaned.

"It won't do you young ones any harm to stop those fizzy drinks and crispy snacks," she said. "In my young day you were glad of the school milk, and we would have thought we were in heaven if someone had offered us an apple or a banana. We came to school with cold toast wrapped up in newspaper."

I don't think Betty was old enough to have lived such a hard life, but she was a kind lady and we all loved her. She always wore a jet black wig under her white cap. Rumours were rife that she had had a strange illness and lost all of her hair. But Betty once told us (that's me, Holly and the Twins) that she could never be bothered going to the hairdresser's, so she wore a wig to save herself the trouble. Secretly, I wished she would book a visit from my mother (a mobile beautician) because I think her wig, as my gran might say, has seen better days. (She has a funny way of speaking, my gran, but I love her just the same.)

Betty, along with every other member of staff in the school, remembered Angela as a pupil. She had a photographic memory when it came to pupils, but could never remember the prices of the food and drinks in the cafeteria. It's just as well for her that the tills were electronic and that the pupils all had cards which our parents would credit each week, for our lunch and interval snacks. Even then Betty had difficulty swiping the cards through the machine. What is it with older people and technology? You would think sometimes that they were dealing with monsters from outer space that had come to catch them and whisk them off to their spaceships.

Mind you, my Grandma Winters is the exception to that rule. She may be ancient, but she knows how to text and e-mail and when there's nothing good on the telly or she's fed up with her DVDs and music, she shops online. She says that the internet's the best thing since sliced bread, whatever that means.

Anyway, we sat around the cafeteria eating our healthy lunch of tuna pasta and low fat strawberry yoghurts. We were joined by Andrew and Paul who spent most of the time flicking through the holiday photos on my mobile phone and contributing very little to the conversation.

Holly said, "I see Bella has two new people to order about. When did Jade and Danielle become so friendly with her?"

"Bella doesn't really have friends," said Debbie.

"No, just people who are easily ordered about," said Louise. "I just hope it means she will leave everyone else alone."

Bella had picked on the Twins quite a lot since she came to our school. She saw them as an easy target because they were so nice and friendly and even wept buckets if someone stood on a spider.

\*\*\*

I was dreading going back to class after lunch, even though the fuss about Angela had died down. Everyone else seemed to have forgotten she was my sister. Or so I thought ...

We were all working quietly on the – you've guessed it – *Summer Holiday Essays* when there was a fit of giggling and whispering coming from Andrew's and Paul's group. I wasn't facing their part of the class, so I couldn't see what was happening. Angela was busy taking down some old posters and replacing them with brightly coloured posters of places we had visited on the cruise. I heard a voice hissing, "Naw, you ask her. Go on."

Then I definitely recognised the next voice. It was Paul Rankin.

"Please, Miss. Please Miss Winters, see that poster of Minorca you've just put up – is that – is that where you wore your *bikini?*" Before he had finished the question, the other boys in his group fell about laughing, and then the whole class was buzzing with the boldness of the question.

Angela's face went as pink as her blouse. She was speechless for a moment. Just as she was about to reprimand Paul and the others, Ms. Snodgrass walked into the mayhem. Before you could say *Ms. Snobby* the noise had stopped. Except for the sound of a thud. Something had dropped on the floor beside Paul's group. Paul made to bend down and pick it up.

"Just leave it, young man!" snapped Ms Snodgrass, and she glided over and picked up *my mobile phone!* She

22

looked at the phone, looked at my sister, and then ordered Paul to stand outside her office. And I knew why. I had forgotten that in amongst my holiday snaps was a photo of Angela sunbathing in her bikini!

Now half the boys in our class and Snobby Ms. Snodgrass had seen it too!

I was afraid to look at Angela. Beside Ms. Snodgrass she looked like a little school girl again. She didn't get a chance to deal with the situation because *Ms. Snobby* told the class to get on with their work, glared at Angela and asked me to follow her to her office.

My first day in Primary Seven and I was already in trouble and all because of a stupid photo.

Paul was already standing nervously outside *Ms. Snobby's* Office when I arrived. I thought she would be right behind us, but she had probably decided to give the rest of the class an extra row 'just for good measure' (another one of my Grandma's sayings). I stood beside Paul, but deliberately kept my eyes averted. It was the only time that day, when I was angrier with someone other than Angela.

"I'm sorry, Sam," whispered Paul. "I didn't mean to get you into trouble. It was just a bit of a laugh."

"Some laugh!" I retorted. "We'll probably get detention for the whole of our P7 year."

"Do you really think so?" he said, the panic evident in his voice. "That means I'll miss football practice ..."

"You div!" I said, "Do you believe everything you're told?" I didn't get a chance to say anymore because the clip-clopping of *Ms. Snobby's* heels echoed along the corridor, and she was soon standing over us, with her dark eyes boring into us and her red lips parted like a tiger about to devour its prey.

"This is not a promising start to your final year. Samantha Winters, you know the rules about mobile phones. They are to be used only during lunch and intervals and *never* in the classroom. As for you, young man, your impertinence towards Miss Winters deserves a phone call to your parents." Paul's face turned white at the thought of his parents becoming involved. But, *Ms Snobby* was in an unusually good mood because she sent us back to our class with a stern warning that a repeat of such behaviour could have *serious repercussions.* We didn't know what *repercussions* looked like but we understood the word *serious* and felt relieved that our ordeal was over. Well, Paul's was; I had to return at the end of the day and collect my mobile phone from her office.

When we slipped back into the classroom, everyone else had obviously been so impressed by *Ms. Snobby's* warning that they didn't even look up, but kept writing furiously. As for me, the enthusiasm for writing about the cruise had evaporated and I churned out a half-hearted effort which didn't do justice to all that we had done and seen.

But, as far as I was concerned, that was just another thing which was Angela's fault – not mine!

# Chapter 3

## Trouble (7 Letters: 4 consonants; 3 vowels)

The bell signalling the end of the day couldn't come soon enough. I was out of the classroom and zooming homewards like a hare which has been let loose from a trap. I even forgot to collect my mobile phone!

I threw open the garden gate, kicked it shut, opened the front door and closed it with a bang. I fired my school bag onto the floor in the hall, almost knocking over the brolly stand, flounced into the lounge where Grandma Winters was engrossed in her daily dose of *Countdown,* flopped onto the sofa and grunted as loudly as I could.

"Had a nice day, Samantha dear?" Gran said as she concentrated on making a word out of a bunch of mixed up letters. "*Dumpling* – that's eight letters," she said proudly to the television set. "That's my score up to 32, and it's only the end of part one." She wasn't really speaking to me. She talks out loud when she's watching the telly. She hadn't even noticed that I was in distress, fit to burst.

"Had a nice day? Had a nice day? You must be joking, Gran. This has been the worst day of my life!" I said fighting back tears of anger and frustration.

"Don't worry, pet," she soothed, still concentrating on her notepad. "The first day is always the hardest after a long summer break. It'll be better tomorrow. You'll see."

"I won't be going back to that crummy school tomorrow or any other day!" I wailed.

But, my complaints couldn't compete with Gran's telly programmes, especially *Countdown*. At any other time, she would have been extremely sympathetic, but I had been pushed aside for a bunch of letters and numbers. I could be weeping buckets and she would finish her words or sums. Words and sums! That just reminded me of school and Our Angela.

I went to my room determined to shut myself away and starve, so that I would be too weak to attend school the next day. In fact, a hunger strike was the perfect solution: I wouldn't have to face Our Angela over the dinner table or listen to her prattle on about lessons and weddings and getting me into trouble over the mobile phone fiasco. Problem solved.

Well, until the delicious aroma of Gran's cottage pie wafted upstairs, under the doorway straight to my nostrils. She had promised strawberry trifle for pudding too, because it was our first day back. My tummy was rumbling louder than a train thundering along the track near our house. It was difficult to be strong on an empty stomach. Starvation was all very well if I had a stash of crisps and drinks to fall back on. (Okay, so that would be cheating, but I never said I was a noble type of person like in the stories we read at school.)

I was just about to sneak back to the lounge when I heard the front door slam and Our Angela's voice screeching, "Where is she? Wait till I get my hands on her! I've never been so humiliated!" I had never heard

Our Angela shouting like that before. It was quite scary. I closed my door quietly. There was no way I was going back into the lounge, not when Our Angela was like that – not even for Gran's delicious cooking.

Besides which, I knew exactly what she would be telling Gran, and Mum when she came home, and I wasn't ready to face their disapproval too. I thought of sneaking out and running away to Blackpool to join Dad on his coach tour. (His job since he was made redundant from the bank.) I even contemplated dressing up in one of Gran's outfits with matching walking stick, and passing myself off as one of his *Old Dears*. (Dad's nickname for the pensioners who booked the tours.)

But that would only cause more trouble what with police searches, helicopters out scouring the land, Mum and Gran making tearful pleas on the telly – all because of a little photo on a mobile phone. As far as I was concerned, this was Our Angela's fault for getting a job in *my* school and ruining my hopes of a blissful final year. Nope! If anyone was going to run away – it would have to be Our Angela! With these brave thoughts, I opened the bedroom door and boldly made my way to the dinner table where Gran had already served up the piping hot cottage pie.

Mum and Angela were already at the table. Angela's eyes were red and puffy, as though she had been crying. Grandma sat down and said "Bon Appetito" in a strange foreign mix of French and Italian, trying to bring a smile to the stony faces sitting around the table. We started to eat, the only sound in the room that of our knives and forks chinking against the plates.

Normally our meal times were full of chatter and laughter. This was so bizarre. I had eaten a few mouthfuls but found difficulty swallowing, even after sips of water. I just didn't have any appetite. It looked as though I was going to starve after all. Out of the corner of my eye, I could see that Angela was shifting her food around the plate, without actually lifting any to her mouth. Grandma was the only one who seemed to have a hearty appetite. But she always said that 'if you had to live through war and rationing, you would never waste good, wholesome food'. Not that she said anything on this occasion; she knew, as she might say herself 'when to hold her peace'.

I so wished that Dad had been there – he would have kept the conversation going. I don't know whether or not I would have preferred Mum or Angela to have a go at me about the mobile phone, and then it would have been out in the open and over with. This silence was deafening and bad for my digestion. The last time I remember feeling as bad as this was when Mrs McNulty announced her retirement.

It suddenly hit me! Mrs McNulty, whom I adored, had actually caused this situation. If she had worked on till her *real* retirement age, Angela would have gotten a job at another school and then everyone could have tucked into Gran's cottage pie with gusto and laughed and joked about *first days back*.

Somehow, that thought didn't make me feel any better.

Now, I know what you're thinking. You're saying to yourself: *how could she not know that her own sister was coming to teach in the same school?* Well, perhaps you have a point. But, just think about that last week of the summer break – playing out with friends, lazing about watching DVDs or listening to your iPod. Time flies. You don't really take account of all that is going on around you. And, let's face it – even after six weeks holidays – SCHOOL is the last thing on your mind!

Still, now that I do think about it – well I'm not eating my dinner, so I might as well think about it – Angela *did* get a strange phone call about a week before school began. I remember her yelling and screaming and kind of jumping about the room, a huge smile on her face. I thought it was something to do with the Engagement or the plans for the Wedding. (That kind of thing always sends Our Angela into raptures.)

But, later that day, I would see Mum and Gran, huddled together in whispered conversations, looking at me, and then nodding their heads. That evening, when Rob, Angela's fiancé came round, the process would be repeated by them. I went to my room and looked in the mirror. I thought maybe I had come out in blotches or perhaps my hair was sticking up, or falling out, leaving bald patches. Nope! I looked as normal as I had ever looked. Then, as suddenly as I had noticed their strange behaviour, I had forgotten about it.

That surely must have been the day Angela found out about Summerlee Primary, and everyone had neglected to tell *me* about it!

"You should have told me," I blurted out, my mind firmly in the flashback, my body still at the dinner table, "about Our Angela coming to Summerlee Primary!"

"Perhaps we should have, dear," said Mum, "but that's not a reason for deliberately embarrassing your sister on her first day at her new job."

"Oh it's always about *her* in this house! What about *my* embarrassment? It was my first day too – in Primary Seven!" I cried, tears welling up. I left the dinner table, knowing that whatever I said, Our Angela would get the sympathy while I got all of the blame.

I kept to my room and I was left alone 'to cool down' as I could just imagine my Mother saying. I didn't want to be there when Rob came round to see Angela. I didn't even leave the room to speak to Dad when he phoned. I thought I could get back to him on my mobile, but then I remembered it was lying in *Ms. Snobby's* desk drawer in school. Towards bedtime, I did accept hot chocolate, digestive biscuits and a cuddle from Mum.

But I went to sleep determined about one thing: Our Angela would be sorry that she came back to ruin my last year at Summerlee Primary!

# Chapter 4

## Talks, Tantrums and Teething Troubles

Before I knew it, two whole weeks had gone by and Our Angela was still our classroom teacher; she was still engaged to Rob, the Dishy Dentist; and she still talked non-stop about wedding plans, though only when she wasn't talking about *lesson plans*. Yeuch! The boys in the class were still hanging on to her every word; and the girls were constantly quizzing me about where she bought her clothes and jewellery. Even Holly and the Twins, – my best friends in the entire world – thought Angela was a fashion icon!

How was she ever going to give up on Summerlee Primary with wall to wall adulation like that?

It was a lovely sunny September morning, spoiled only by the fact that we were stuck in school doing a science project. I hated science, and maths and anything really that wasn't creative. I usually relied on Debbie and Louise, the Twins, who were both excellent at those subjects and didn't mind helping me out. We had to do an experiment and while the Twins were working away, I kind of daydreamed that I was climbing trees in a sunny forest. (We don't have any sunny forests in Summerlee; in fact there are hardly any trees or sun, but there's no harm in imagining, is there?) Anyway, I had just reached the top of my imaginary tree and was about to do a daredevil jump across to another tree when I was startled by a yelp.

Debbie was clutching her hand which looked red and bruised, while Louise and Holly were comforting her.

"What's up?" I said, "Something go wrong with the experiment?"

"No," whispered Holly, "the experiment was going fine. Bella has pinched our stuff and she's going to pass it off as her own. Debbie tried to stop her, but she scratched her hand."

It was just our luck that Angela was going round the groups and had stopped at Bella's before I got a chance to retrieve our materials. Angela studied the experiment, her face beaming.

"Well done, Bella, Jade and Danielle! You must have worked very hard on that experiment. That's certainly worth a Gold Star and points towards your Golden Time at the end of the week."

Our group was next. I could see Bella and her cronies sniggering as they knew that we hadn't time to come up with new results. Angela's face fell when she saw our messy table, and Holly and the Twins frantically trying to put things right. I was too busy glaring at Bella and mouthing "I'll get you for this." to contribute. Angela noted our failure to succeed with the experiment on her clipboard.

"Better luck next time girls," she said comfortingly to Holly and the Twins, seeing that Debbie was in tears and assuming it was because the experiment had gone wrong. "Perhaps next time, Sam, if you contributed more instead of gazing out of the window, the experiment would work. It is, after all, supposed to be team work."

I didn't know who deserved my deadly stare more – Our Angela or Bully Bella. I hadn't been much use to Holly, Debbie or Louise during our science project, and I felt guilty that I had been responsible for points being deducted from our Golden Time. I was more concerned with getting to the interval and getting even with Bella and her cronies.

Revenge on Our Angela could wait till later.

The morning interval finally arrived and I set off looking for Bella, not quite sure what action I was going to take. It always looks good on kids' TV when the heroine (or hero) takes on the bully, wins and everyone cheers. Real life isn't like that. I knew that Bella would be up for a fight; fighting is her favourite hobby. But, to tell the truth, I'm not really a fighter. I mean, I don't go round the school or my street at home looking for people that I can beat up. But, I felt that I had to make Bella see that she couldn't steal other people's work and think she could get away with it. Otherwise, there would be no stopping her.

I thought of telling Angela the truth of the situation, but things were still rather frosty between us since that first day. Besides which, she had praised Bella loudly in front of the rest of the class, so she couldn't very well go back to her and take back the Gold Star and the points. Angela would see that as a weakness, making her look foolish in front of the whole class. I'm not even sure she would have believed me anyway. She would probably think it was another plot to make her look bad. Normally, I quite like the idea of Angela looking bad and then hopefully looking for another job, but I wanted to protect my friends from Bella more than I wanted to embarrass Angela.

So, there I was at one end of the playground staring over at Bella and her cronies, ready to rush over and punch her lights out. (If my Gran could hear me even thinking phrases like that, she would be in shock! It's certainly not a phrase you would hear in her collection of funny sayings. My Gran hates violence. She says that 'two world wars were fought to end violence, not make people more violent'.)

Just as I was about to make my move, I saw Holly and the Twins walk up to Bella, and speak to her. Holly looked to be doing most of the talking while Debbie and Louise cowered behind her trying to look brave, but not exactly pulling it off. The next thing I saw was Bella pushing Holly backwards so that she almost fell on top of her schoolbag which did land on the ground. When Holly bent down to catch her bag, Bella kicked her in the ankle. I could see the pain on Holly's face, as she tried to fight back tears. Meanwhile, Jade and Danielle, Bella's cronies, towered over the Twins, making sure that they could do nothing to help Holly.

News of a playground fight spreads faster than the flu' virus and I had to battle my way through a crowd to get to Bella. By the time I reached her my blood was boiling and I felt myself grab Bella's hair and swing her 'round till she was dizzy and screaming for me to let go. Bella is a dirty fighter – she scratches at the face and eyes, kicks and punches like a wild animal. She was pulling at my blazer, trying to wrench my hands from her hair. But I was like a lioness trying to protect her young. (Well, I know I'm the same age as Holly and the Twins, but you get my meaning.) I could hear the excited voices of the crowd surrounding us, some chanting for Bella, but most of the voices for me. (Bella had bullied a lot of people in Summerlee and they would be glad to see her getting a taste of her own medicine.)

But the taste of victory didn't last for long. The crowd's voices became fainter in my ears. Neither Bella nor I had noticed that the Teachers had arrived like the Cavalry did in the old Western films that my Grandpa Winters used to watch. Mr Bamber and Ms Snodgrass parted the crowd and came towards us, Mr Bamber catching hold of my blazer, while Ms Snodgrass pulled Bella away from me. Bella's hair was standing on end; she looked as though she had stepped out of a horror movie. Her face was red and puffy, and I imagine that I looked like a ragged orphan from a Victorian novel.

"This is *not* the behaviour of young ladies," said Mr Bamber in a very serious-but-don't-mess-with-me voice, "and certainly not what I expect to see from some of our senior pupils." He let go of my blazer and turned to the very silent crowd which only a few moments previously had been urging us on. "You will *all* make your way to your classes, where I suggest your teachers might set you an essay on 'The Importance of Responsible Behaviour'. Ms Snodgrass, I will leave the two culprits in your capable hands and trust you to devise a punishment which will give them time to reflect upon their conduct."

"Before the boys and girls return to their classes, I think Isabella and Samantha should shake hands and apologise to each other and to the rest of us for spoiling what had been a very pleasant interval," said Ms Snodgrass with a voice as cold as ice cubes.

Bella and I scowled at each other, while the rest looked on in silence, wondering if another fight was about to break out. I was determined not to be the first to stretch out my hand; after all, this was Bella's fault for pushing my friend. Then I saw Our Angela, at the back of the crowd, looking so embarrassed and guilty as if she, and not me, had been the one in a fight. So, I stuck my hand out at Bella and mumbled "Sorry," and she, looking smug that I had made the first move, looked straight at me and said, "Sorry too," with a total lack of sincerity.

The crowd of onlookers shuffled off to their classes and Bella and I were about to follow when Ms Snodgrass piped up, "Not so fast, girls. I haven't finished with you yet. Shaking hands was the easy bit. For the next week, you two will spend part of your lunch break cleaning up the school grounds as part of the Eco Project. *Together!*"

*Ms Snobby* was right. That did make shaking hands seem such a doddle. A week in Bella's company filled me with horror. And I could see by the look on her face that she wasn't exactly thrilled either. *Ms Snobby* escorted us back to the classroom, looking rather pleased with herself, while I contemplated the idea of lunchtimes with Bella and missing out on fun times with my friends.

I didn't speak to Bella during that first lunchtime. We spent the whole twenty minutes or so in sullen silence as we made our way around the playground picking up litter with the grabbers the Janitor had provided us with. We had two separate bin bags – one for stuff which could be recycled such as plastic bottles and paper items; another bag was used for the rest of the rubbish, mostly uneaten food. I have to say I was gobsmacked at how careless people were and how much food was wasted. I had never really noticed it before. I suppose, too, I was concentrating more because I was determined not to look at Bella, let alone speak to her.

Of course, Holly was in floods of tears for the rest of the day, because she felt so responsible for my punishment. To think I had fought Bella to save Holly from being hurt, but she ended up crying just the same! She cheered up in the afternoon, however, when Angela went over the plans for our Health Day. The following morning, Rob, Angela's Dentist fiancé was coming to the school to talk about taking care of our teeth. He was going to have a job on his hands – I had seen the mountain of sweetie wrappers and empty fizzy drinks cans we had bundled into refuse bags that lunchtime.

And that was during only *one* lunchtime!

Our class spent the afternoon setting out the Assembly Hall for Rob's Talk and demonstration on how to brush our teeth properly. We helped Angela to put up bright posters and set up the smart board and equipment, so that everything would run smoothly. This presentation had been Angela's idea and she was doing everything to make it a success. Of course, she had plenty of eager helpers from our class, both boys *and* girls. Mr Bamber popped in with Ms Snodgrass. He looked very impressed and complimented Angela on her organisational skills, but the only comment I heard Ms Snodgrass make was for Angela to make sure that all mobile phones were switched off. I saw the look she gave Angela and when my sister blushed at the reference to *that incident*, I almost felt sorry for her.

At home, she didn't tell Mum or Gran about the Bella Incident – I think she wanted to keep me in a good mood in case I took it out on her when Rob was in the school. She can be quite crafty, can my sister, when she puts her mind to it. And it suited me that I wasn't in my parents' bad books. Well, mostly it was because it was Gran's Baking Day, and I didn't want to miss out on her scrumptious apple and cinnamon pie with custard by being forced into another hunger strike. Besides which, Mum was over the moon about having 'landed' a walk-on part in an episode of Gran's favourite cop show, *"Taggart"*. She was to be 'on set' very early next morning, before the birds were even up. "I hope I get to be in a scene with DS Jackie Reid – she's my favourite," said Mum. "I wonder what they'll want me to wear. I expect it will be outdoor clothing. I think it's a street scene."

Mum talked about these walk-on parts as if she was a major star in the production, and kept recordings of all of the programmes she had 'appeared' in, even when she was simply a dot on the horizon. Still, it kept her happy and sort of made up for the fact that she never got to fulfil her dream of being a make-up artist to the stars. Mum's philosophy was that you should never give up on your dreams – just like I was never going to give up on my dream of getting Our Angela to move to another school, so that I could enjoy the remainder of my Primary Seven year in peace!

Mum was off in search of TV stardom by the time I surfaced next morning. It was only Gran and I for breakfast. Angela had also left with the larks to help Rob prepare for his debut. He might have been safer with criminals on the set of '*Taggart*' than trying to convince an unruly bunch of kids that *toothpaste* was preferable to *toffees*.

Rob may be the dishiest looking dentist for miles around, but he doesn't really know how to relate to kids. And he does go on and on about healthy teeth and gums. He can't switch off, even when he's not at his surgery. Every time he comes to our house, I get a lecture on what to eat and drink and what to avoid.

"All things in moderation, Sam. You can have the occasional fizzy drink, but always remember to use a straw." Now, if I had 10p for every time Rob said that to me since he started dating Our Angela, I would be able to buy a whole van load of fizzy drinks, with or without straws!

Everyone in our class, especially the girls, was excited about Rob's visit – not because they were keen on healthy teeth and gums, but because they would get to see Miss Winters' fiancé. Actually, it all went rather smoothly. Rob spoke very quietly at first, but as his talk progressed and he could see that the pupils seemed interested, he became more confident and his voice became stronger. I could tell that Angela was trying not to draw attention to herself by concentrating on working the technology, but she looked very proud of Rob.


When he had finished speaking, Rob asked if there were any questions. A few of the younger pupils asked what was the best toothbrush to use and how often should we visit the dentist. He dealt with these questions easily and then a voice cried out, "Have you seen Miss Winters in her bikini?" History was repeating itself. The girls started giggling, the boys joined in, and I didn't dare look at Our Angela or *Ms Snobby*. Poor Rob! His face went red as a bowl of beetroot and all his confidence disappeared as he stuttered and stammered and tried to recover his composure.

Mr Bamber, the Head Teacher, stepped onto the stage and immediately the Hall fell silent. He said that he was ashamed of the behaviour of a few immature pupils, but he would find the culprit and she would be very sorry she had interrupted such an interesting and beneficial presentation. Why did he so confidently say *she* and not *he*?

Then I saw *Ms. Snobby* speaking to Angela and pointing to the back of the hall where I was sitting.

The voice had come from *our* row. Bella, who was sitting right next to me, had been fidgeting and yawning during the whole presentation. She had tried to bully Paul and Andrew into shouting out about the bikini, but they were having none of it so, for once Bella did her own dirty work and shouted out herself. *Ms Snobby* ordered our class to remain seated while the rest were dismissed for lunch. She stood over us like a towering giant. She was very blotchy, which spelled trouble because she only got like that when she was *very* angry.

She looked along the row of girls. *Ms Snobby* had a way of making you feel guilty even when you hadn't done anything wrong. The only one who didn't fidget or blush was Bella. That should have been a sign to *Ms Snobby* that she had her culprit; instead she looked directly at *me* as she spoke.

"I don't need to tell you how disappointed Mr Bamber and I are with the conduct of this class so far this term. I would hope that the culprit would own up and save the reputation of those who are innocent." I nudged Bella but she ignored me and didn't make any move to stand up and confess.

"Very well," said *Ms Snobby*, "I have no choice but to remove Friday Golden Time for the next two weeks – for the whole class."

Everybody loved Friday Golden Time. It was the last hour of the week, and if we had been good for the whole week, we got to choose how to spend that time from a range of activities: computer games, board games, drawing and painting or reading. Any pupil who misbehaved or didn't work hard throughout the week had minutes deducted from their Golden Time. For the *whole* class to lose *all* of their Golden Time was *mega serious*!

There was a muttering and grumbling as boys and girls hissed at Bella to own up, but she didn't flinch. Now, there was no way anyone would give Bella's name – they were too scared of her and no one likes to be called a 'grass'. I could see that *Ms Snobby* was running out of patience, but Bella didn't budge an inch.

There was nothing for it. I stood up. "It was me, Miss. I – I did it."

There were gasps from Holly and the Twins, and mutterings from the boys. *Ms Snobby* had a glint of a smile on her face as she said, "I should have known it would be you, Samantha Winters. You seem determined to be the class clown this year. Your yard cleaning will be increased from one week to two weeks."

Then we were dismissed.

\*\*\*

It was bad enough coming home from school when I knew I was in trouble with Angela, but I was dreading the fallout after the Rob Incident at school. Now I had two angry faces staring at me across the dinner table – Angela *and* Rob. Gran was oblivious to what had happened and carried on dishing out our meal as though everything was 'hunky-dory' (another of her mysterious catch-phrases).

"So, everything went well, Rob dear, at the school?" she said, not noticing the daggers which were zooming towards me from Our Angela's eyes. Not wanting to cause a scene in front of Gran, Rob said politely that everything was fine and then changed the subject by complimenting Gran's chicken casserole before he had even put a morsel in his mouth. I hated the fact that they made me suffer by *not* saying anything about the day's events. I just wanted *one* of them to blame me for another disastrous day in their lives and then I could get on with sulking *and* eating.

But the accusations didn't come and the anger and guilt I felt were welling up inside me like a can of juice which had been shaken and was bursting with fizz. In the end, fizzing mad myself, I stood up and couldn't help myself shouting across the table at Rob.

"I'll eat as many sweets as I like and drink as many fizzy drinks as I can swallow in one gulp and there's nothing you can do about it! So there, Rob McGregor!"

Angela was about to speak, but I had started and I couldn't stop. All of the frustration I had been feeling since that first day came pouring out. "As for you, Miss Goody-Goody Gumdrops, it's bad enough that you're my teacher and I have to put up with you at home and school, but *he's* not my dad and he can't tell me what I can and can't eat." There was a stunned silence. Angela's face drained of colour and Rob looked even more embarrassed than he had earlier that day at school.

Just then, the front door opened and Mum came breezing in. "Guess what! I got to be a psychiatric nurse and wear a uniform and everything."

"Just as well, Sandra dear, because it's been like a lunatic asylum here," said Gran in her matter-of-fact voice. "Would you like some chicken casserole? Everyone else seems to have lost their appetite."

# Chapter 5

## Halloween's for Wimps!

After Rob's almost disastrous visit to the school and a telephone telling off from Dad, I kept a 'low profile' as they say in Gran's cop shows. Even Bully Bella was keeping quiet. I had tried to get through our playground-cleaning punishment without speaking to her, but she wore me down with her attempts at conversation. She even apologised for not owning up to the shouting incident at Rob's presentation. She said she would have been expelled after that incident, because she had been on a final warning from Mr Bamber. I wasn't surprised that Bella could be sent to yet another school, but I was gobsmacked at her apology. I had never *ever* heard Bella apologise to anyone, even teachers. Perhaps she was beginning to change. Perhaps there was a good side to her after all.

It was a relief, however, to get the punishment over with and get back to the lunch time routine of going to the school cafeteria with my friends, Holly and the Twins. They didn't believe me when I told them about Bella's apology.

"What's that saying we learned the other day?" said Holly. "A leopard never changes its spots."

"She's certainly as scary as a leopard," cried the Twins in unison.

"And why is she always coming up to you at the interval, all buddy-buddy?" said Holly as she bit her way into a tuna sandwich. "I preferred her when she was nasty. At least we knew where we were with her."

I was upset at the reaction of my friends, but of Holly in particular. "I've seen a different side to Bella during these last few weeks. At least she understands what I'm going through with Our Angela," I said quite huffily.

"Bella got you into trouble at the presentation, not your sister," said Holly. "And I don't understand what your problem is. Miss Winter – I mean – your Angela is a fabulous teacher."

"Yes, so she is," agreed Debbie and Louise piped up with, "She's letting us get dressed up at Halloween and we can make up witches' spells and stories on the smart board."

"Yeah, well at least Angela won't need any make up or costume – she's already a witch!" I retorted feeling irritated that no one saw Angela the way I did.

"That's really cruel, Sam," said Holly, and the Twins both nodded in agreement.

My feeling of missing my friends had evaporated. I picked up the remnants of my lunch and took it over to the plastic bins provided. Bella, who was sitting with her two sidekicks, Jade and Danielle, signalled to me to come and join them. I hesitated for a moment, then, thinking it would teach Holly and the Twins a lesson, sauntered over to Bella's table and sat down.

"We were just talking about Halloween," said Bella. "We're thinking about going out guising on that new estate beside yours. Do you want to come?"

I was taken aback by the sudden invitation and I could tell by the stunned look on Jade's and Danielle's faces that they were surprised too. They even stopped chewing on their bubblegum for several seconds – a record for them. Jade and Danielle didn't say a lot, but they made up for their lack of conversation with plenty of chewing.

"Thanks," I said, "but I go guising every year with Holly and the Twins. It's a kind of tradition."

"Tradition? What's that?" said Danielle to Jade who looked as puzzled as her pal.

"Tradition," said Bella "means it's *boring* and Sam needs a change. What about it, Sam?"

"I'll give it some thought, Bella and I'll get back to you," I said as the bell sounded for the end of lunch. I felt relieved. It was one thing talking to Bella during school time, but I wasn't ready to socialise with her outside of school.

At least, that's what I thought ...

\*\*\*

The Friday before Halloween was Angela's much talked about '*Dress up and tell a story day*.' Everyone in the class was really excited, even the boys, who would normally consider '*dressing up*' to be a '*girly thing*'. The idea was that everyone wore a costume and made up a story behind the character of the costume. Each person would tell a story to the group, with the best story in each group being presented to the class. There was a great variety of costumes – most probably hired or bought from the Party Shop in the Precinct in the centre of Coatbridge.

Holly dressed up as Cinderella in her rags, (before she went to the Ball to meet Prince Charming). The Twins, Debbie and Louise, dressed as the Ugly Sisters from 'Cinderella', though I wondered how they were going to get through *one minute* as two of the nastiest characters in Fairy Tale Land, never mind a *whole day* at school. They were more likely to let Cinders go to the Ball and pay for her outfit and carriage as well!

There were several Harry Potters, at least half a dozen witches, two Sleeping Beauties complete with designer pyjamas and tiaras, several Super Heroes, and Paul and Andrew had come as two Pirates of the Caribbean. Even Bella and her pals had found costumes (or stolen them from *Ms Snobby's* wardrobe, as Andrew and Paul suggested). Bella, unsurprisingly, had dressed as Cruella de Vil from *101 Dalmatians* while Danielle and Jade were dressed in fluffy Dalmatian pyjamas and slippers. Bella joked that the other 99 Dalmatians were at home. No one laughed except Danielle and Jade. No wonder – Bella looked even scarier as Cruella than she did in her own clothes.

Of course, Our Angela had to join in the fun too.

"I can't ask the pupils to do something I'm not prepared to do myself," she said, as she stitched silver wings onto the back of a shimmering sequined ballerina gown the night before – she would be the Fairy Godmother to Holly's Cinderella. Holly would love that! Angela looked as though she had just walked out of a Hollywood film, and didn't the kids in our class just love her even more.

As for me, I didn't tell Angela what I was planning to do on the day. I just turned up in my school uniform. I wasn't going to give Angela the satisfaction of thinking she had won. I still wasn't going to make it easy for her.

46

But, I didn't calculate how I was going to feel as the odd one out amongst all of those fabulous costumes, the *most* fabulous and the *most* admired being – Our Angela! Of course, one silly person had to ask me, "What have you come as, Sam?" while some smart kid replied with, "The Naughtiest Girl in the School."

This time, everyone did laugh!

Angela offered to let me go home and change, but I made the excuse that I was feeling unwell and asked to be sent to the school nurse. I wasn't really ill, but I was close to tears. I just couldn't bear to see everything going well and to see everyone drooling over Angela. I heard later about the fabulous stories which were made up including an update of the Cinderella story which found Holly's character, Cinderella, turning up to the Ball in a stretch limo, and Bella's character, Cruella deVil, being hypnotised and joining the RSPCA. Angela had provided Halloween Trick or Treat bags for everyone and there was singing and games.

I couldn't sort out my feelings. I wasn't sure if I was disappointed at missing all of the fun, or if Our Angela was deliberately trying to show me up in front of my friends. Either way, I couldn't bear the thought of listening to Holly and the Twins going on and on about it while we were out guising, so I decided that I and my Witch costume would join Bella or Cruella instead!

# Chapter 6

## "Dirty Tricks and Treats"

It was an ideal night for guising or 'Trick or Treat' as everyone seems to call it now. It was pitch dark just before 6pm and there was a crisp frost which made the ground all silvery and sparkly like icing sugar on a sponge cake.

I was a bit of a coward because I had texted Holly instead of telling her in person that, for the first year that I can remember, I wouldn't be sharing Halloween with her. I didn't want to get into another row about Angela and have my best friend defending my worst enemy – my big sister. I didn't let Mum or Gran know that I was going guising with Bella, Jade and Danielle. I quickly did a twirl in my costume and left the house before they could ask too many questions. I deliberately chose a witch costume because I didn't want anything too girly.

Secretly, I wished I was a *real witch*, so that I could cast a spell on Our Angela and turn her into a toad. There was no way Rob would walk down the aisle with a toad and that gave me double satisfaction – I could ruin her wedding *and* her teaching career at the same time. I did my best witch cackle at the thought of that.

Yes, in that mood and with those wicked thoughts, I was definitely cut out to be a witch and I couldn't be in better company than with Bella de Vil and her cronies, Jade and Danielle. It started off ok. We went round the houses on our estate, carefully avoiding my own house and Holly's. I was glad, too, that we didn't bump into Holly and the rest of my friends on the way round, though I did spot them in the distance, laughing and giggling and having a good time.

I thought being out with Bella would be fun, but her kind of fun wasn't mine. I was used to going to houses and using the old Scottish intro: *"The sky is blue, the grass is green, please can I have my Halloween,"* then singing a song or telling a joke. Bella simply said in that gruff voice of hers, *"Trick or Treat"* while Jade and Danielle, chewing gum as though their lives depended on it, thrust out their carrier bags and shook them cheekily until something was put inside. They didn't even have the good manners to wait until the door was closed before moaning about the lack of sweets or crisps and tossing apples and nuts – the traditional *treat* – into unsuspecting gardens.

I was glad when we had tried all of the houses on our estate and moved into the next estate where I was less likely to go to the houses of people who knew me. The houses on this estate were much larger than ours – mainly detached houses with expensive cars parked outside. I think people on this estate deliberately left their cars parked in the open to show off to their neighbours. Jade and Danielle thought it was funny to sit on the bonnet of one of the cars and bounce up and down till the alarm went off. When I told them to stop it or we would be in trouble, they simply sneered.

"Oh, we'll be in trouble! Oh, we're so scared!" then fell about laughing. I think they would have been more suited to the witch costume than I was. Bella joined in their laughter.

"That's more like it girls. Now we're having some *real* fun."

"We're supposed to be guising, not vandalising people's property." I said. "Let's just stick to that."

But, I had hardly finished speaking before Bella blocked the path of a group of guisers dressed up as aliens. Bella towered over them looking menacing, while Jade and Danielle grabbed hold of their bags and emptied the contents onto the pavement. They rummaged for sweet, crisps and juice and stuffed them into their own bags and then made off down the street leaving the kids in floods of tears. I stood like a statue while all of this was going on. I hesitated, wanting to help the aliens put the stuff back into the bags, then I heard Jade yelling, "Sam Winters, get a move on or you'll be caught!"

Now that my identity was revealed, I hurriedly set off after the others. I hadn't done anything wrong, but I felt guilty just the same. I had seen Bella in action plenty of times at school, but this time I seemed to be on her side, not the side of one of her victims. I felt sick as I ran after Bella and the others. Luckily for me, they had disappeared by the time I got to the end of the avenue, so I made my way home.

I slipped quietly into the house. The television was quite loud, so I knew that Gran and Mum would be watching their Soaps. I flopped onto the bed, too tired and miserable to take off my witch costume, or remove the green make up which came with the outfit. I must have dozed off because I didn't hear the doorbell, or the shouts of Mum and Gran from downstairs. Next thing I know, Mum is peering down at me, and shaking me. I woke up and rubbed my eyes.

"Young lady, get yourself downstairs this instant. There's someone at the door for you."

I was still a bit sleepy, but I followed Mum downstairs and was met by a stern looking Gran, who turned to a figure at the door and said, "This is Sam, my grand-daughter, but I think you must be mistaken—" Before she could finish, a young voice coming from an alien costume screamed, "That's her, Mummy, she was with the bad girls who took our Trick or Treat Bags!" I could feel the blood draining from my cheeks even under the thick, green gunge which covered my face.

"I don't know what you're talking about," I muttered unconvincingly. "I've been out all evening, and I'm not long back." The mother of the alien held out a canvas carrier bag full of Halloween Goodies, pointing to a label on the inside of the carrier. I looked at it reluctantly and noticed Gran's name and our address on a label sewn onto the canvas. The woman said, "Since I think it is unlikely that this elderly lady (pointing to Gran) would be out guising, then this must be yours." She thrust the bag into my hands and continued, "You and your friends are very lucky that I didn't call the police. Children should be able to go out guising without bullies like *you* attacking them."

Gran was about to have a go at the woman for calling her *elderly,* but not before Mum apologised and said that they would punish me and make sure such a terrible thing never happened again. She transferred all of my goodies into another bag and made me hand them to the tearful alien to make up for the stuff which had been stolen. Once the alien and his mother had been satisfied that I would never cast another spell, at least on the streets of Summerlee, Mum was able to close the door and I was able to go back to my room. Well, not quite straight away.

"You've got a lot of explaining to do, young lady," said Gran.

"I just can't imagine Holly and the Twins bullying other children and taking their treats," said Mum.

"Oh, and I suppose that means you think I could!" I said, feeling hurt that I wasn't included in Mum's list of unlikely criminals and that they didn't even give me a chance to explain the way things really happened.

"And don't think the punishment ends with the lost treats," continued Mum. "You'll be grounded for a week."

"I didn't want the lousy treats anyway," I said fighting back green tears. "Nobody likes stupid apples and nuts anyway!" I stormed upstairs, even more upset that I was beginning to sound like Bella. That was the second time Bella had been bad and I was the one who took the blame.

"Well, you'll not want any more of my apple and cinnamon sponge then," said Gran before I slammed shut the door of my bedroom. Trust Gran to know how to get to me. I could stand being stuck in the house for a whole week. That way I wouldn't have to face people at school when word got around about my encounter with the aliens, *and* I could avoid Bella making any more brilliant suggestions for getting me into trouble. But a *whole week* without Gran's baking – now that was real torture!

By the time I could be bothered having a shower and washing off the witch make-up, Angela was home and no doubt hearing about my 'latest exploits' as Gran called it whenever I got into trouble, which seemed to be just about every day recently. I stopped at the top of the stairs to listen out for my name and Angela's reaction. They were speaking quietly and the television was back on. All I could make out was Angela saying something about "now the trouble is spreading outside school, that's worrying." I could just imagine Angela worrying about *her* reputation and hoping that I wasn't going to do anything to embarrass her in or out of school. Well, I made up my mind there and then that I wouldn't be around to embarrass her – I was going to run away!

These thoughts are great when they pop into your head because you immediately think of films and television programmes where the put upon heroes and heroines come up with all sorts of devious plans and carry them out without a hitch. Then, the people who have upset them come to their senses and welcome them home with open arms and humble apologies. Yes ... that's what happens in the world of television and film ... but this was Summerlee and I didn't have a ghost of a plan!

I flopped down on the bed, throwing my discarded Halloween costume onto the floor. Then, it hit me like a thunderbolt! Halloween! Costumes! Disguises! I wouldn't run away as ME – *I would go in disguise*! I flopped again, punching my already battered pillows. *What disguise?* I couldn't use my witch costume since it was not really the ideal outfit for blending into the background. I was mentally running through and discarding a list of possibilities, when Gran's voice intervened, calling me downstairs for cocoa and cheese on toast.

Thunderbolt Two hit me – *Gran*! Gran with her oodles of outfits and walking sticks for every occasion. I would dress up as an elderly lady and escape on one of my dad's *Old Dears' Tours.* (Of course, I had conveniently forgotten that this plan had occurred to me that first day back at school, when Our Angela had turned up as our teacher. And I had also pushed to the back of my mind the reason I *didn't* go ahead with the plan – police helicopters and tearful television pleas by Mum, Gran and probably Our Angela.)

But, this time I was desperate and this was my only hope of escape.

# Chapter 7

## Wigs and Walking Sticks...

I only had a few days to prepare before Dad's next trip. Fortunately, he was leaving on a Saturday morning, and not a weekday, so there would be no chance of Angela missing me when she called the class register. Saturday mornings were also good because Mum was very busy with her mobile hairdressing business, Angela was doing wedding things with Rob, and Gran liked a lie-in. I was used to getting my own breakfast and heading off to the Heritage Park or playing football in the park with Paul and Andrew.

I had been careful not to get into any more trouble. Instead, I became really helpful about the house tidying up, washing up, hoovering – anything that would allow me to go in and out of rooms without drawing attention to myself. I had managed to sneak an outfit complete with matching walking stick from Gran's room and stashed the 'loot' in the bottom of my wardrobe along with a wig and make-up from Mum's work stuff. I only took make-up items from her old stock and there wasn't really much call for the wigs – unless she needed one for her walk-on work. Sometimes I would get pangs of guilt – sneaking about the house like a burglar, becoming as scheming as Bella. Perhaps I was turning into Bella?

I thought of the times when I was little and Gran would play dress up games with me – and here I was playing the game for real. But, I was determined to go through with my plan. They would all be sorry for nagging me and making my life a misery. It was time for me to teach *all* of them a lesson!

I was *so* feeling sorry for myself.

*** 

The Saturday of my Big Plan dawned and I had no time for second thoughts. Dad's bus was due to leave Hamilton at ten o'clock and I had to be dressed and hide in Dad's car before he left for the bus station. In addition to my 'costume', I had borrowed a very old fashioned looking weekend bag, nicknamed Gran's *Mary Poppins' bag* by my dad. I stuffed it full of sweets, crisps and cans of juice – Gran would have a fit if she saw what I had put together as breakfast. I also crammed in some magazines to read during the journey. I made sure they were Gran's – I think the other old folk on the trip might be suspicious if I started reading girly comics. I was quite proud of my planning. Mum couldn't be better prepared for one of her acting jobs!

I took one last look in the full length mirror before tip-toeing downstairs and out of the house, as I thought, for the last time. I looked spookily like Gran. My face was partly hidden by a wide-brimmed hat, with the grey curls of the wig just visible enough to show my 'age'; the make-up, I hoped, would add to the impression. I wondered if I had gone too far with the ruby red lipstick, but that was Gran's favourite colour, and anyway there was no time to remove it and replace it with a paler colour. I had remembered to wear gloves to hide the fact that my hands were those of a young person and not a seventy-something pensioner. I was very proud of my attention to detail.

Now all I had to do was get into Dad's car without being spotted. I heard him whistling – another habit which annoyed Mum but one which I like because it meant he was happy. I imagined him whistling when he got over the shock of finding me at Blackpool, pleased for once that he had some familiar company on the trip. I soon came out of my daydream when the whistling stopped and I knew he would be going out to the car. I opened the front door of the house and peeked out to make sure that none of the neighbours were taking advantage of the early morning sunshine to wash cars. Earlier, I had heard Dad putting his luggage into the boot of the car, so I knew it would be unlocked. I sneaked inside the back of the car and lay down on the floor, being careful to stay still. I had been to Hamilton many times and knew the journey only took about fifteen minutes. I don't think I had stayed still for fifteen minutes during my whole life but I couldn't mess things up now! He got into the car, whistling again, and adjusted the mirror. It seemed to take forever before he turned the key and the engine burst into life, but it did and we were off.

It was an uncomfortable, bumpy journey but it was taking me to Blackpool with my dad and leaving all my troubles behind in Summerlee. I felt like whistling too, but old ladies don't ... do they?

As we drove into the Bus Station, I felt my stomach do summersaults, and I thought I might have to throw up but, my determination to get on that bus made me swallow hard. Instead I had to concentrate on getting out of Dad's car with my luggage and without him spotting me. This was harder than I thought. I felt a draught as he opened the boot to get out his holdall. Just as I was about to sneak out of my hiding place a voice called out to him. Fortunately for me, the person who had called to him seemed to have come towards him and they stood at the boot of the car moaning about the passenger lists not being printed off and how that was going to hold them back.

This was my chance to escape. Dad hadn't closed the boot and this became my camouflage. I squeezed open the passenger door and slid awkwardly out onto the ground, dragging my bag behind me. I found myself in a car park at the side of the bus station, reserved for the workers. Luckily there was no one else around. I picked up my bag and walking stick, held up Gran's long skirts and quickly sprinted for the toilets where I could check that my disguise was still intact. (I had been getting some strange looks from passers-by. Then it dawned on me – I was supposed to be an elderly woman but I was running like an Olympic sprinter.)

Back outside, I scoured the bus terminals till I saw the sign for 'Blackpool' and noticed that a large queue had already formed. I almost giggled as I surveyed the crowds searching for the 'blue rinses' which Dad had often joked about. Actually, I didn't see anyone with blue hair, but some rather sprightly pensioners who had an air of mischief about them which reminded me of some of our school trips – though thankfully I didn't spot anyone who could be an Elderly Bully Bella.

Up until this point, my plan was going very smoothly – too smoothly! I spotted Dad, loading luggage into the back of the coach, then back to the queue and checking pieces of paper before taking the next piece of luggage and placing it expertly beside the others. Those pieces of paper must be important – they must be a kind of passport onto the bus. But, I didn't have one and even if I could produce one, I didn't want to get too close to Dad before I even had a chance to board the bus.

I decided to wait until Dad was busy loading his next suitcase and climb onto the coach, making sure to sit at the very back where hopefully I could 'keep a low profile' as the criminals often said in Gran's crime dramas. I was beginning to feel like a real criminal, and I didn't like the feeling at all.

I was glad of the commotion of people settling into their seats or trying to heave coats and carrier bags onto the overhead racks as I stumbled along the narrow aisle of the coach. Luckily, not many passengers were making their way to the back of the bus, so I found a seat easily and settled in by the window. I placed my *Mary Poppins* bag on the seat beside me, in the hope that no one would then attempt to join me. As the time drew closer to the departure and I gazed out of the window at the crowds milling about the bus station, I felt the confidence I had experienced earlier disappear like the sun which was just slipping behind grey clouds.

I was jolted out of my day dreaming by the sound of the engine. This was it! In a few moments we would be off and I would officially become a *runaway*. Then I saw Dad get up from his seat, leaving the engine purring while he made his way up the aisle, clutching a sheet of paper and counting heads as he made his way towards the back of the coach and – *me*. I slid down in the seat, burying my head in *The People's Friend* – a magazine which was Gran's favourite and apparently read by women of a certain age up and down the land. Of course, I wasn't interested in its content, but it did cover my face effectively till thankfully Dad passed my seat and made his way down the aisle to the front of the coach. He scratched his head, looked at the piece of paper, looked up and down the coach and scratched his head again.

To my horror, he started to count the heads again, and I slid so low in my seat that I almost ended up under it! In my efforts to remain hidden, I knocked Gran's walking stick onto the aisle almost tripping up Dad as he did his serious head count.

"That's a fine walking stick," he remarked as he picked it up. "You don't often see that shade of red. My mother has one just like it." I muttered "Thanks, Son." I kept my head firmly behind the magazine as I stuck out a gloved hand to retrieve the walking stick. But Dad was still studying it and seemed reluctant to hand it over.

I peeked out from the corner of the magazine and caught him eyeing his list, then the seat number, then the walking stick, then me – or at least what was visible. Still clutching the walking stick, he asked if he could see my ticket. The magazine was trembling now as my muffled voice replied, "I think you took it earlier, Son, when I boarded the bus."

"I would have given it back, Madam, and I certainly would have remembered that striking outfit..." he said as he gently removed the magazine to get a better look at my face. "Do I know you, Mrs...?"

"Mrs Snodgrass" I said unconvincingly, as I had plucked a name from the magazine, the first name which caught my eye, "M-Mrs -eh – Morag Snodgrass. Yes, that's it. That's my name, Mrs Elspeth Gillespie ... I mean, Mrs Morag Elspeth Gillespie."

"Well, Mrs *Gillespie,*" said Dad, though I'm sure with a hint of a smile. "The numbers on the coach don't seem to tally with the numbers on my computer list, so I'll have to check *all* of the tickets again, and I may as well start with yours since I'm at your seat."

My cheeks were burning up with embarrassment. There was a buzz of chatter as people looked round the coach to see what the commotion was, or stood up to get a better view. I was sure that Dad had recognised me so why didn't he just come out and say it? Then as if he had read my mind, Dad leaned across the seat as though to hand back the walking stick and hissed in my ear, "What do you think you're doing, Sam? Did you think I wouldn't recognise my own mother's walking stick, clothes and bag?" Then he stood up again and spoke in a loud voice as though he wanted the whole of Hamilton, never mind the people on the bus to hear what he had to say.

"Oh dear, Mrs Gillespie, your ticket isn't for this coach. Why don't I help you off with your stuff and we'll get you on the correct coach?"

I'm sure that Dad was just trying to save me further embarrassment, but I was livid that my escape plan had been foiled just when I should have been on my way to freedom. I wasn't going to give in so easily! I said in my loudest voice, "I'm not leaving the bus, *Dad!* I'm not going back home to Summerlee where everybody hates me. I'm running away with you to Blackpool!"

This outburst caused quite a commotion amongst the other passengers. I heard someone mutter that this was better than watching the soaps. I also heard someone else remark that I must be senile if such an *old lady* was calling the coach driver 'Dad'. But, I remained glued to my seat, arms folded and refused to budge. Dad said, "Look, Sam, all of these people have paid good money for their holiday, and if I don't get on the road soon, we'll be late getting to the hotel and their holiday will get off to a bad start."

"That's right," I said huffily, "you care more about your passengers than you do about me!" I knew that wasn't true, but I just couldn't help myself.

Dad got out his mobile phone and called Mum to come and collect me. Now, I was beginning to feel really uncomfortable. Mum would have to leave clients in mid-beauty treatment to make the journey from Summerlee to Hamilton. What if she was in the middle of giving someone a perm and their hair turned frizzy and she was sued or struck off the Hair and Beauty Association – if there was such a thing? It also occurred to me that Dad might get into trouble, especially if the passengers started to complain.

There was no sign of that really. There were a few mutterings and grumblings, but old folk just seem to take things in their stride and so they used the extra moments to get tucked into their homemade snacks or to read their newspapers or magazines or make yet another trip to the toilet. In fact, one old biddy had the cheek to ask for my *People's Friend* magazine since I obviously wouldn't be needing it now.

For the first time since I had formed my *Escape from Summerlee Plan,* I thought of the consequences: Mum and Dad disgraced, without jobs, perhaps even without a home if they were sued; me taken into care because they would be blamed for my attempts to run away; Gran forced into an Old Folks' Home; and Our Angela permanently mortified and probably abandoned by Rob the Dentist because he could not risk marrying into such a notorious family. I was forming quite a list. In fact, it was so dramatic that TV producers would probably be falling over themselves to make a reality programme ...

Now, my dad doesn't do angry. He's the kind of person who sees the best in people, but I could see that the whole situation was upsetting him. I remembered how sad and quiet he was when he was made redundant and how some of the fun left him. Then, when he found a new career driving holiday coaches, not only was he back to his old, happy self, but he really and truly enjoyed his work. He said when he had finished a tour, he left his work behind in the bus depot, unlike his job at the bank where he was always worrying about targets and statistics and bringing briefcases full of papers home – and here was I about to be responsible for losing this job.

"Come on, pet," he said softly, "time to go home." With tear-filled eyes, I sniffed all the way down the aisle, following Dad like a lost puppy, but with my costume now trailing the floor, my hat and wig lopsided, I looked more like an abandoned rag doll.

Once outside the coach Dad put his arm round my shoulder and tried to point out the dangers of what I had done.

"You can't just run away every time you have a few problems, Sam. I mean, slipping out of the house like that, without telling Mum or Gran – think of how worried they would have been when they couldn't find you." By the end of this speech I was howling. Passers-by looked astonished to see this 'old lady' apparently being told off by a coach driver. It's a wonder someone didn't call the police to have Dad arrested for harassing the elderly. Dad gave me one of his huge cotton hankies and I blew my nose loudly which drew even more curious stares.

"I-I'm s-sorry, Dad," I stammered between sobs, "I just didn't know what else to do."

"Take up acting," he said with a twinkle in his eye, "you look really good in that costume. Just the spitting image of your gran, right down to the ruby red lipstick."

I was beginning to feel a bit better till I spotted Mum's van turning into the bus station as though she was taking part in a high speed chase. (It's a wonder she wasn't arrested too.) Somehow, I knew the lectures wouldn't be over just yet. Mum would have her say, followed no doubt by Angela. And I dreaded to think what Gran would say when she saw I had taken her best outfit and her precious *Mary Poppins* bag. Yet, I didn't say a word all the way home. I let Mum remind me of the worry I had caused, and the danger I had been in. "Who knows what might have happened if you had got lost in Blackpool – it doesn't bear thinking about."

At home, the expected rows from Angela and Gran didn't materialise. Perhaps Dad had warned them not to, or perhaps they could see by my tear-stained face that I had learned my lesson. Or perhaps they were secretly relieved that I had chosen Dad's bus to stow away on. Either way, I was glad to be home again. I had been stupid and silly, but I promised Mum and Gran that I would never be *that* stupid or silly again. (Somehow they didn't seem to be convinced.)

I apologised to Dad when he phoned to say they had eventually arrived at their destination in Blackpool. He said that the passengers on the coach thought it was the most entertaining start to a journey they had ever had; in fact some of them thought it was a stunt for one of those reality shows where people are set up by friends or family. Apparently, Dad wasn't the only one who thought I had a future in television or in the theatre or that this incident was worth its own TV slot.

\*\*\*

Later that evening, Gran and I had the sitting-room to ourselves while Mum and Angela made wedding plans in the kitchen. Gran had made her famous hot chocolate and we sat cosily by the fire, one of her favourite Shirley Temple movies playing in the background. (Believe it or not, this movie was called 'Stowaway'. The main character, however, was hiding out on a passenger ship heading for the Far East, not on a package bus tour to the North of England.)

Gran didn't approve of what I did, but she did see a funny side to it.

"When I was your age," she told me, "the Second World War had just started and I thought of running away to be a spy. I thought it would be easy to find a plane and a parachute and be dropped somewhere in France. At that time I didn't know the names of any towns or villages there, but I imagined that I would return to Scotland to be presented with a bravery medal." She sighed and sipped her hot chocolate. "I never did get my adventure. Instead I left school at fourteen and started work in the Co-op. Still, it wasn't all bad, because, a few years later, that's where I met your Grandpa when he came home on leave from the Army."

\*\*\*

Isn't it strange how when you are young, you always want to look *older,* but when you get to be Mum and Gran's age, you want people to think that you are *younger*?

# Chapter 8

## Guy Fawkes must have met my sister!

Now, I know what you are thinking: surely she must have received some sort of punishment for the trouble she caused, almost running away and getting everyone into a flap? You're thinking perhaps I was fined a year's pocket money? Or perhaps, doing the washing up for *two* years – *without the aid of a dishwasher*? What about washing Mum's van once per week for *the rest of my life*? Any one or all of these would have been preferable to what really did happen – being enrolled for ballroom dancing lessons! And on Saturday mornings too! My Mum called that poetic justice. I mean, what's poetry got to do with it?

A few days after *it* happened, Mum came bouncing into the house after work, beaming as though she had just won the National Lottery. One of her regular clients has a son who is in my class at school. His name is Dennis Grant and he's one of those boys who is almost invisible. He is really brainy, but doesn't show off. Any teacher we've ever had knew that if a question was asked – on any subject – and the rest of us didn't know it, then Dennis could be relied on to provide the correct answer. He was brilliant at tests and always good when a visitor came to the class and Mr Bamber, the Head Teacher, wanted to impress.

Well, apparently Dennis is a Brainbox *and* a Brilliant Ballroom Dancer. He has won zillions of medals and trophies, but his partner, Temara, had the cheek to emigrate to Australia (with her parents of course) and Dennis was on the lookout for a new dance partner.

Now, in the winter months when, as Gran would say, 'the nights are fair drawing in', Saturday evenings when *Strictly Come Dancing* and the *X-Factor* are on, are telly heaven for Mum and Gran. (And to think that adults say that children spend too much time in front of the telly!)

Surely my mum didn't think *she* could be Dennis' partner? And, although Gran had lots of experience watching dancing in her ancient *Fred and Ginger* movies, I think her walking-stick might just get in the way. (Gran said that Anton du Beke and his professional partner, Erin Boag, are a modern day Fred and Ginger.) Obviously, I'm no brain box, because it took a while for me to realise that Mum had actually put *me* forward as a partner for Dennis. Gran said it would keep me out of mischief and I would be learning a new skill. She said it would 'kill two birds with one stone' – another one of her funny sayings, though why she should use that example I don't know, because my Gran wouldn't hurt a fly.

So, before you could say 'One, two, cha, cha, cha,' my Saturday mornings were taken up with quicksteps and waltzes and jives and Dennis moaning about how hard it is to 'break in a new partner' and how he would probably 'never ever again win another competition'. Honestly, Dennis might be as quiet as a mouse in the classroom, but when it comes to the ballroom, he could teach Bella a thing or two about bullying. Oh, and if you thought that was bad enough, Our Angela and her fiancé Rob the Dentist were going to be 'escorting' me to and from the McKinney School of Ballroom Dance in the centre of Coatbridge. Angela had decided that she and Rob should get in some dancing practice before the wedding. Super great! Now, as well as Our Angela bossing me about during the week at school, she was going to be ordering me about on Saturday mornings as well. I did consider taking my case to the European Court of Human Rights, but since I hardly made it out of Hamilton on my dad's coach, the chances of me making it to Europe were virtually a big fat zero!

School wasn't much better. Once Halloween is over, it is straight on to projects about Guy Fawkes. We get it every year from Primary One straight up until our last year. No doubt, we will go through it all again when we go to High School. Our Angela said that since we were the oldest pupils in the school, we should study the dangers associated with this time of year and make posters and leaflets to be put up around the school and distributed to our younger pupils.

Our project was to be called 'Fire, Fireworks and Bonfires'.

We were going to study actual newspaper accounts of accidents which had occurred through misuse of fireworks and not paying attention to proper supervision of bonfires. Mr Bamber had arranged a visit by the local Fire Brigade, who were bringing a real fire engine into the school grounds. The Fire Safety Officer would judge our posters and the winner would get a Family Pass to the organised fireworks display at Summerlee Heritage Park, which was always spectacular and usually sold out very quickly. For the past few years, my dad hadn't managed to get tickets, so we had to be content with watching the display from my parents' bedroom window. We had a good enough view, but it wasn't the same as actually being in amongst the crowd and the excitement of it all.

I was torn between wanting to make the best poster and not wanting to make Angela look good if I won the prize. I was feeling a bit left out in our class group, because Holly and the Twins were not really speaking to me after the Halloween snub. They didn't ignore me completely, but they left the class quickly at intervals and lunchtimes and I took the hint that they didn't want me around. That meant I was forced to hang around with Bella and the Terrible Two, Jade and Danielle. They weren't much friendlier. They told me off for not running away from the *aliens* and said if I had been caught it was my own fault – I should learn to run faster.

On the day of the visit by the Fire Brigade, Bella was absent. It wasn't an unusual occurrence for Bella. She had been known to skip school and forge her own absence notes. On this occasion, Jade was quick to point out to Angela that Bella had caught a tummy bug and wanted to be at home close to a toilet. The phrase 'too much information' sprang to mind, but that was Jade, looking round to see who was blushing or smirking or both. Angela was (unfortunately for me) getting better at dealing with these incidents and ignored Jade's remark, instead setting everyone to the task of displaying their posters.

I had been put into Bella's group to help Jade and Danielle finish off their posters. We were all excited about the visit of the Fire Brigade. We were to be given a talk and then get to climb up onto the fire engine, try on helmets etc. I was really looking forward to it, so I was desperate to get Jade and Danielle's posters onto the wall, afraid we would be left in class and miss the fire engine fun. Then, Danielle said she wasn't feeling well, that she probably had the same tummy bug as Bella. Jade was still adding bits to her poster, so I was told to take Danielle along to the toilets. I offered to stay behind instead and finish Jade's poster but, for once in her life, she seemed keen to finish a piece of work.

As we made our way along the corridor, Danielle suddenly stopped her moaning and groaning and grasping her tummy and practically skipped into the loo.

"There's nothing wrong with you!" I exclaimed.

"So!" said Danielle who whipped out her comb and proceeded to fix her hair.

"So," I said, "we'll miss the talk by the Fire Safety Officer and a chance to go on a real fire engine."

"Big wow!" Danielle sneered. "I don't know how I'm going to cope."

I decided to wash the poster paint off my hands so that our trip wasn't entirely wasted. I removed my blazer and turned on the taps. By this time Danielle had switched her attention from the mirror to the window which overlooked the senior playground. It seemed a bit pointless to me, because the bottom half was frosted glass. Danielle climbed onto the radiator, which fortunately wasn't very warm. These old radiators were seldom roasting hot, despite our school Janitor, Bill Watson's best efforts. He said the boilers were as old as the school itself and should have been replaced long ago. Bill seemed to have been at the school for as long as the boilers, 'man and boy' he told us. I think he has as many crazy sayings as my Gran.

By the time had I had scrubbed my hands and tried to dry them with the yucky paper towels, Danielle had jumped down off the radiator and seemed anxious to get back to class. Just as we were about to leave, Danielle bent down and picked something up from the floor.

"Look what I've found. Some div has dropped a couple of bangers on the floor."

"Someone must have brought them in and thought better of it with fire fighters in the school," I said. "We had better hand them into the Office on our way back to class."

Danielle threw the bangers at me as though they were red hot.

"Well, you take them and put them in your pocket. I'm really scared of fireworks." And before I had time to protest, she had dashed out of the toilets and was heading back to class.

We had to cross the playground to get back to our block. Danielle kept looking at her watch then looking over towards the bicycle sheds which were situated beside the school gates. Of course, safety regulations meant that the school gates were locked while pupils were in class. Today, however, the gates had been left open to allow the fire engine to drive into the school grounds.

Something caught my eye – a shadowy movement by the bicycle sheds. I thought at first someone was trying to steal one of the bikes. Then I saw feathery blue smoke, heard a hissing sound followed quickly by several loud bangs. Danielle screamed like a banshee and ran for cover behind a bench. I was about to join her when I saw a figure come out from behind the bicycle sheds and dart out of the gates. I was sure I recognised the figure. It was Bella!

I turned round to ask Danielle if she had seen what I had seen, but she had disappeared. Next thing I find I'm in the middle of the playground with Mr Bamber, *Ms Snobby* and a tall man in a fire fighter's uniform storming towards me. The fire fighter checked the bicycle sheds and made sure they were safe. He was carrying something in a bucket. I couldn't see what it was, but there was a strong burning smell – the gunpowder aroma of fireworks. He had sprayed foam into the bucket, but, the fireworks had all gone off before they had arrived on the scene.

The fire fighter looked very stern when he addressed Mr Bamber.

"Someone has been setting off *bangers* – the nastiest of fireworks if they get into the wrong hands. The culprit obviously thinks this is a joke. It's a lucky thing it wasn't at interval or there could have been a nasty accident." He was speaking to Mr Bamber, but the three pairs of eyes were firmly fixed on me. Then it dawned on me. I was in the playground when the fireworks went off.

They thought I had done it!

I felt the colour draining from my face. Here I was feeling guilty for a crime I hadn't committed. But, at least I had a witness. Danielle had been with me when the banging noise sounded from the direction of the bicycle sheds. She must have seen the figure running out of the school gate – even if she didn't recognise it as Bella. I plucked up the courage to speak, even though I felt my legs shaking and my palms were all sweaty.

"Mr Bamber, Sir, I saw someone running out of the gates just after the banging noise. I was just about to run and fetch someone, when you all arrived."

"How very convenient, Samantha Winters," said *Ms Snobby* whose blotches were particularly *blotchy* at that moment, "and did you happen to recognise this intruder?"

"Yes, Miss, it was Bella Hendry, Miss," I said confidently. I had no qualms about telling on Bella on this occasion. We had been told enough about the damage caused by careless use of fireworks and how it was too serious to protect those who didn't worry about the dangers caused to others. I was feeling quite bold and proud of the fact that I had been around to witness such a serious crime, so I piped up with:

"You should be able to catch Bella's image on the school CCTV and her DNA is bound to be on the used fireworks." (The DNA remark was thrown in to impress the Fire Safety Officer. I had watched lots of *True Crime* programmes with Gran and knew all the tricks of the forensic trade.)

My remark, however, didn't appear to have the desired effect. The three adults looked at each other and I'm sure I saw a smirk on their faces which they tried hard to hide since it wouldn't have looked very good to be smiling during such a serious situation. Instead of being thanked for my information, I was sent back to class.

I walked in feeling very pleased with myself. Everyone crowded round me asking what had happened and if anyone had been arrested yet. Of course, when the bangs had been heard from within the building, pupils got over excited thinking it was a bomb or at the very least an earthquake. Angela had a hard job getting everyone back to work. We had our break in class instead of going outside. Danielle was summoned to the Head Teacher's office and was away for what seemed ages. When she came back to class, she looked tearful and wouldn't speak to anyone, not even her best buddy,

Jade. She wouldn't even look at me, though I tried desperately to catch her attention to find out what she had told Mr Bamber.

All of the fun that I had been looking forward to didn't materialise for me. We did get our talk from the Fire Safety Officer, Gordon Dempsey, who pointed out the dangers of the morning's incident to the whole school this time and not just to me, Mr Bamber and *Ms Snobby*. Of course when he said that the culprits, once caught would be severely dealt with, there was a lot of nudging and whispering and shuffling round in seats to look at me and Danielle, but mostly at me. The poster competition was won by a pupil in one of the junior classes, but the biggest disappointment for me was that while our class got a turn on the fire engine I was summoned to Mr Bamber's office.

I just assumed that he was going to congratulate me on my powers of observation, but I was thinking as I walked along the corridor towards his office, that he could have waited till the fun was over. Then, it occurred to me that I might get a special award of tickets to the Heritage Park Fireworks Display after all. Perhaps I would get my photo plastered across the front pages of the local newspaper. Perhaps the Mayor of Coatbridge would present me with a medal for good citizenship. I smiled at these thoughts of possible glory as I knocked confidently on Mr Bamber's door. I grinned as I heard the word, "Enter," and I bounded in to the room.

As soon as I saw the frosty expressions on the faces of Mr Bamber and *Ms Snobby* my dream of fame fizzled into a horrible nightmare. *Ms Snobby's* blotches betrayed her anger. Mr Bamber always looked serious so it was difficult to detect his mood at all. I felt so small standing across from them, even though they were both seated.

Mr Bamber cleared his throat and began the interrogation.

"Young lady, this morning's incident has shown Summerlee Primary School in a very bad light, on a day when we *should* have been leading lights in the community." (So far, I hadn't a clue what he was on about and why he should keep mentioning lights all of a sudden. And if there had been a power cut and there was no light, shouldn't he be interrogating an electrician?)

He eventually said something which I couldn't help but understand – he and *Ms Snobby* had discovered that Danielle and I were the only two pupils out of class at the time of the *incident*. That meant we were the only pupils who could have had access to that area of the school grounds near the bicycle sheds.

"You were also found to have several of the offending fireworks on your person," he said, "so all of the evidence points to you having set off those fireworks. What do you have to say for yourself?"

Actually, I couldn't say anything for several seconds. I was speechless. When I recovered, I managed to remind them that I had seen the *real culprit*, and that it was Bella Hendry. I also told them that Danielle was with me at the time and she must have seen her too. *Ms Snobby*, who had kept unusually quiet up until this point, seemed anxious to speak.

"As it happens, Samantha, we checked your little tale regarding Bella. I phoned her home and was informed by her mother that she was safely tucked up in bed."

"She only lives about five minutes from the school, Miss," I said. "She could easily have slipped out and been back home before her mother noticed she was missing."

"I hardly think that would be likely, particularly since she is suffering from a nasty tummy infection," said *Ms Snobby*, totally rejecting my suggestion.

"Danielle saw her too. She was with me in the yard. And *she* was the one who found the fireworks on the floor of the Senior Girls' toilets!" I said triumphantly. "She knows that the fireworks were never mine in the first place."

"Ah," said *Ms Snobby* as though she was a lawyer in a courtroom. "Danielle. It seems that she didn't notice any movement in the area of the bicycle sheds, that it was too dark to see anyone who might be lurking there, and that she was too scared of the banging noises."

"As for the bangers found in *your* possession," continued Mr Bamber as though he and she were part of some kind of double act. "Danielle seemed to think that you had brought them with you to school and that you had been keen to show them off to her when you visited the lavatory." (*Lavatory?* Where did he get that word from? It was like something Gran would conjure up for her *'Countdown'* programme.)

"Well, Danielle's a liar!" I protested, feeling the tears welling up in my eyes. I could see a different kind of headline in the local newspaper now: TEACHER'S SISTER IN FIREWORKS FRAME UP! Then, a light went on in my head. Perhaps the scandal would be enough to get Angela the sack or perhaps she would be so embarrassed that she would resign. Just as I was getting accustomed to the sacrifice I was about to make – taking the blame for a crime I didn't commit – I caught the tail end of Mr Bamber's speech.

"... and so when pressed further, Danielle admitted that it was *she* who found the fireworks on the floor, not you, but she still insisted that she could not identify the real culprit ..."

*Ms Snobby* escorted me back to the classroom. They only had *circumstantial evidence*, but she and the Head Teacher still thought I was somehow involved in the firework incident and couldn't be trusted to wander about the school alone. Outside the classroom, *Ms Snobby* gripped the door knob tightly as she peered right into my eyes, "Don't think you have gotten away with anything, Miss, or that having a sister who is a teacher in the school will prevent you from being punished properly in the future." Then she opened the door and sent me inside. The room was empty and I could only witness the fun people were having on the fire engine from the window of our classroom.

I had time, though, to think over the situation I had found myself in. Bella was supposed to be helping me get rid of Our Angela from Summerlee Primary, but the only person who was likely to be thrown out was me! What was Bella up to? How was I going to concentrate on Angela, if I had to keep my other eye on Bella? There would be fireworks when Bella got up out of her phoney sick bed and returned to school. I wasn't scared of Bella, but now I was sure that I couldn't trust her.

# Chapter 9

## Parties, Presents and Christmas Crackers

I couldn't believe it was December until Our Angela brought a huge Advent Calendar into the classroom, and promised that each pupil would get a chance to open a window and sample the chocolate delights hidden there. I wasn't worried about when my turn would come around; I was just disappointed that another month had come and gone and my sister was still my teacher!

At home, Dad was around more often during the week. Winter months meant fewer tours; instead he did daily journeys to Edinburgh, Aberdeen or Perth. It was great to see him every evening and listen to his tales of life on the road with coach loads of his 'Old Dears'. Of course, he daren't use that phrase around Gran, his mum.

'You're only as young as you feel, Arthur, my boy, and you're never too old for a telling off!' she would say to him. I mean, my dad – a *boy*? Mum says that parents always think of their offspring as children, no matter what age they might be. I hope I don't develop these strange attitudes when I'm an adult. I'm sure I won't.

Of course, Dad tried to be the peacemaker between Our Angela and me. He must have had a headache listening to our complaints about the school situation. He said he could see both sides, and that we had to make the best of it. He told me that I was very lucky to have a sister who was a teacher and could help me with my homework, since she would be setting it. He understood it was an unusual event, but since none of my friends seemed to be bothered or treat me differently, I didn't really have much to complain about.

Inside, I was disappointed that he didn't rush straight up to the school and order Mr Bamber to remove Angela from my class, but I didn't want to upset him on the few occasions when he was at home. He gave up, however, trying to get me to see things from Our Angela's point of view – as a teacher new to the job and faced with a younger sister in her class. I just wasn't prepared to look at things that way, at least not yet. I just wanted to enjoy Dad's company and visits to the Heritage Park, rides on the tram followed by cinema trips and eating out.

At Dad's request, however, I did accept Angela's offer of a girly trip to Glasgow one Saturday, to do some Christmas Shopping and see the lights in George Square. Mum and Gran seemed relieved that I had agreed to the idea without creating a fuss. Little did they know that I was relieved to get a day off from my Saturday trips to the McKinney Ballroom Dancing School in Coatbridge and from Denis Grant's moans about my severe lack of dancing skills.

Angela and Rob had given up their weekly lessons, saying that they would resume them nearer the date of the wedding. But, I wasn't allowed to quit, not even when I made the feeble excuse that I was going to be a bridesmaid and would also be busy with wedding preparations. Instead, I had persuaded the Twins, Debbie and Louise, to join the classes too and they absolutely loved it. Unlike me, they displayed some talent; they had what I called *telepathic rhythm.* I asked them to take turns at dancing with Dennis while I was in Glasgow with Angela, so that he might not moan at me as much on my return to the class.

The night before, Mum was remembering her December trips to the big Co-op department store in Coatbridge when, as a young girl, her own mother (now sadly passed away) would take her there to buy her *sticky out dress* for the annual Christmas Party organised by the American firm her own father worked for. She got all misty eyed as she described the silver party shoes with leather soles which made it easy to slide along the dance floor while waiting for Santa Claus to appear down a specially-built-for-the-occasion chimney to deliver the beautifully wrapped presents which were given to each child. Even the party hats were quality, she told us, *and* they received special invitations from Santa through the post.

Angela gave her a hug, despite the fact that Mum had told us this story every year since we were toddlers. "It must have meant a lot to her," Angela told me later. "Remember, Mum was only a teenager when her parents died. It must be difficult for her at this time of year." That was Angela, always understanding 'the big picture' – yet another of Gran's crazy sayings which I love but seldom understand. I don't think it's because Angela is much older than me. I'm sure when Angela was *my* age and Mum told that story she gave her a hug then as well.

Me – I don't do hugs. I just don't do soppy!

We set off for Glasgow early in the morning travelling in by train. It was a crisp, sunny morning and if it hadn't been for the frost whitening the pavements and grass, it would've seemed more like spring. We had both dressed warmly; Angela, as usual, looked stunning, dressed in black jeans, a red duvet jacket and scarlet woollen hat covered in silver sequins, which showed off her blonde hair streaming down her back. She looked too young to be a teacher, but, at that moment, I felt quite proud of the admiring glances she received. Whenever any young man looked *too* admiringly, she was careful to flash her sparkling engagement ring. She usually spent all of her Saturdays and Sundays in Rob's company, so it must have been a bit of a sacrifice leaving him behind in Summerlee to spend a day with me.

The packed train soon pulled into Central Station and I was actually feeling excited about the day ahead. It wasn't just Rob who had been left behind for the day; I felt as though I had left my worries and resentments behind too. I felt like Angela's sister again, and was determined that we would have fun. It would be like old times. And it was.

We started off with breakfast in a little coffee bar in Princes Square. It was choc-a-bloc in this enclosed designer shopping mall. We had hot chocolate and muffins, while carol singers serenaded us from the ground floor. The whole place was lit up beautifully and I felt as though I was in some magical far-off land. We laughed and we giggled at silly things like Angela getting a blob of cream on her nose and me thinking that the Santa Claus in the shopping mall looked like, Bill Watson, our school caretaker. Even that little mention of school didn't dampen my enthusiasm. The comment slipped out quite naturally and there was no tension.

As soon as we had devoured our hot chocolate, we were ready to hit the shops. We had a look round the boutiques in Princes Square, but the prices were as glamorous as the surroundings. We went into all of the boutiques from Buchanan Street to Argyle Street to Sauchiehall Street, stopping only for lunch and coffee. (I should say coffee for Angela and soft drinks for me. I think coffee is yucky!) Angela bought a lovely dress which she said she would wear to our school Christmas Party. Mum and Gran had both slipped me some spending money in case I saw something I liked for the school party. I didn't want a dress, but I did see some sparkly leggings and a cool top which I tried on and thought made me look both trendy and grown up. I had enough money, but Angela insisted I put my purse away, because she was going to treat me.

"I always meant to treat you from my first salary," she said, "but somehow, what with work and the wedding and all, I didn't quite get round to it."

I didn't know what to say. I thought it was too expensive, but Angela insisted. She had always been generous with her presents in the past, but this was different. I had been so mean to her since August, and yet she *still* wanted to treat me. For a fleeting moment I thought it might be some kind of bribe. But, Our Angela isn't like that. To quote Gran again, 'what you see is what you get'.

"Thanks, Sis," I said, and – I just couldn't help myself – I gave her a brief HUG!

On the way back to the station, we stopped off at George Square to watch the skaters on the temporary ice rink. We wanted to have a go ourselves, but we had too many packages and we didn't want to risk losing them. We just stood at the railings, not a care in the world, watching the happy skaters and marvelling at the fact that it had just started to snow! What a perfect end to the perfect day!

But, it didn't end there. When we got home, Rob came round, Dad ordered take-away, and afterwards, Angela and I modelled our new outfits. Later, we all sat down to watch some DVDs. Gran suggested her favourite Christmas Classic *It's a Wonderful Life*, 'a real feel-good film', she said, though we all wept buckets. I'm sure that even Rob and Dad had tears in their eyes. After such a happy, eventful day, life *did* seem wonderful again. But, life isn't like films. Things have a habit of going wrong again. And, for me, they did.

\*\*\*

School in December is usually lots of fun and lots of preparation for having fun. There were preparations for the annual carols' concert, which we usually did for the elderly in our area; there were preparations for the school Nativity Play which the seniors wrote and the juniors and infants performed; there were preparations for the Christmas Parties, including decorating the Assembly Hall and practising the dreaded country dances (well, the boys certainly dreaded the idea of dancing with soppy girls); and there were the secret preparations amongst pupils of what they would buy for their class teacher and who would present it.

I was plagued with requests from Holly and the Twins, about what perfume Angela liked and did I think she would prefer jewellery or should they buy both? Even the boys wanted to know if she preferred flowers to chocolate. I was tempted to tell them all of the wrong things, but I didn't want my friends to think badly of me. I had tried to keep clear of Bella since she returned to school from what I am still convinced was a *fake* tummy bug. She hadn't tried anything recently, but I still didn't trust her. She, Jade and Danielle had refused to give more than a few pence to the class collection for Angela's present.

"She should be buying *us* presents," said Bella, "we're the ones doing all the work."

"Oh, and what would you know about work, Bella, since you never do any?" I said angrily. I'm not sure whether I was angry at Bella for being mean, or for just being Bella.

"Well, you've surely changed your tune, *Samantha* Winters," she said, "I thought you would be the *last* person in this class who would want to buy your sister a present, unless maybe it was a ticket to outer space."

"Very funny, *Isabella* Hendry," I replied in the same sarcastic tone, "but the only person at this moment who deserves a one-way ticket is *you*! So, buzz off and give us peace." Bella saw that I was being serious, so she moved off with Danielle and Jade quickly following her, but the look on her face told me she wouldn't forget this little incident.

\*\*\*

It was the final week before the Christmas break. We had completed our serious work for the term and we were winding down. The Carol Concerts and The Nativity Plays had been performed and pronounced their usual success – what else could you expect when the audiences are full of friends and relatives? All we had to do now was look forward to the end of term party. Angela was allowing us to make our own Christmas cards from old calendars and Christmas cards which we had collected the previous year. This recycling of Christmas materials was also part of our ongoing work as an Eco school.

I had made cards for my parents, Gran and one for Angela and Rob. I couldn't make up my mind what to do for my friends, so I decided to have a little fun and make a joke card and write it from Ms Snodgrass to Mr Bamber. I was quite good at copying other people's handwriting and I had seen enough signatures by *Ms Snobby* to know how to imitate her handwriting. I just had to make sure that I signed it *Ms Snodgrass* and not *Ms Snobby*.

I had chosen an old fashioned Christmas scene, with a couple riding in a carriage, surrounded by snow covered trees. I had originally intended using that picture for Angela and Rob, but had changed my mind. The Victorian outfits suited someone like Mr Bamber, who seemed ancient to me anyway. I put some pink blotches on the cheeks of the Victorian lady to make her look more like *Ms Snobby*. I had just signed the card using a red gel pen, adding a heart and three big kisses, when Angela decided to come round the groups to look at our efforts. I quickly slipped the card into my folder and forgot about it for the rest of that day.

The next day was the day of our party and we were chatting excitedly about what we would be wearing and when and where we would all meet up. The door opened and *Ms Snobby* breezed in clutching a white envelope and looking as red as Santa's outfit, her blotches were so bad. I wondered if she had finally found out something about Bella and had come to expel her. But, when I saw the look of shock and disappointment on Angela's face, I knew it had something to do with me. But what? Since our day out in Glasgow, I didn't have the heart to do anything to Angela, though I still wanted her to leave.

Yet again, I was summoned to the Head Teacher's Office. Yet again, I was facing Mr Bamber and *Ms*

*Snobby*. *Ms Snobby* handed me the white envelope I had seen her showing Angela.

"Open the envelope and look at the card inside, Samantha," commanded *Ms Snobby*. I did as I was told. As soon as I saw the edge of the card and the picture of the couple in the carriage, I knew it was the joke card I had made – but how did *they* get it? The last time I saw it, it had been inside my folder, in the classroom.

"I can see by your expression," said Mr Bamber, "that you recognise this work of art."

"It was only a joke," I muttered blushing with embarrassment.

"I hardly think the message inside the card is funny," Ms Snodgrass said.

"You weren't supposed to see it," I said, hardly able to concentrate on the seriousness of the situation for wondering how it got out of my folder.

"Oh, and I expect that was why you slipped it underneath my door," said Mr Bamber, who had begun to sniff, probably because he was thinking of the message on the card – *Love and lots of Xmas Kisses, from your Darling Principal Teacher, Felicity.*

"I do not know what has come over you, Samantha," he went on, "but it has to be nipped in the bud. You will have to be punished for this incident. What do you suggest, Ms Snodgrass?" (Why could he never think up a punishment of his own?)

She had obviously given it some thought because she immediately piped up with, "I think we shall have to ban Samantha from the Christmas Party." Mr Bamber nodded in agreement, adding: "It is unfortunate to be punishing someone at a time when we should all be rejoicing, but it has to be done. I just hope you have learned a lesson here, young lady. You may return to your classroom."

As I turned to leave, I was about to ask how they knew the card had been written by me, but before I got the chance, Ms Snodgrass handed me a rather sticky lunch card – my name and school photo clear as day.

"This was attached to the back of the envelope. Not very clever of you to leave the evidence, was it?"

I felt like throwing the card back at her, but I didn't have the heart. I walked slowly back to class. I was dreading the hurt and embarrassed looks which Angela would give me and I wasn't in the mood for more interrogation from my classmates. If only I hadn't made the stupid card, I wouldn't be in this mess and I wouldn't be missing the Christmas Party. Angela would probably think I did it deliberately, but why would I want to miss out on wearing my cool new outfit?

As soon as I walked into the room and saw Bella sniggering with Jade and Danielle, I knew she had done it. Somehow she had found the card and slipped it under Mr Bamber's door. She knew that I knew, and that gave her even more satisfaction. She also knew that I couldn't prove it.

At lunchtime in the cafeteria, I was still so angry that I snapped at Holly when she brought up the subject of Angela's present and card. I think it was the word *card* that set me off.

"What's wrong with you these days, Sam?" she said fighting back tears. "You used to be in such a good mood all the time, and now you get cross at the least tiny thing. Surely you're not still mad at Angela? I wish I had a sister like her."

"You can adopt her if you're so fond of her!" I said, without really meaning it.

But this was the last straw for Holly who fought back in a voice so serious it didn't sound like her at all. "Now you're simply being mean and childish. Grow up, Sam, or you're going to be as bad as Bully Bella!" Holly didn't seem to mind that Bella was close by. Even, Mrs Crangle, who was collecting empty tumblers and cutlery from a nearby table, paused to comment.

"Is there something wrong, girls? It's not like you two to quarrel. I mean, it's almost Christmas – peace and goodwill to all men – *and girls*, in this case." And off she went, humming the tune to *We wish you a Merry Christmas*.

I knew that Betty (Mrs Crangle) was right, about Holly and me. We never quarrelled – at least not before this year. So, I told Holly and the Twins about Bella's latest trick and my punishment. Debbie remembered Bella coming to our group to borrow glue on the day we were making cards. She had been rummaging in all of the desks almost daring one of them to challenge her.

"If I hadn't been so scared, Sam, and told her to get lost, she wouldn't have been able to take anything from the desk. I could tell Mr Bamber, though," she said hopefully.

"But, Debbie did you or Louise actually *see* her in the act of taking anything from my tray?" I asked.

"We were too frightened to look at her," said Louise. "We just looked at our work until she went away. I'm really sorry, Sam. It's just not fair that you can't go to the party and Bella can."

"Yes," said Louise, "I've a good mind to boycott the party in protest."

"Great idea," said Holly. "We could start a campaign. Get people in our class to sign a petition."

I was touched that my friends were willing to go to so much trouble for me, but I didn't want their Christmas spoiled as well as mine. That really would give Bella something to gloat over. I had written the card as a joke, and the joke had backfired. I decided to take my punishment and learn the lessons from it. At least one good thing did come from it – I was back where I belonged with my *real* friends and I had Bella to thank for that.

\*\*\*

On the evening of the Christmas Party, Angela looked gorgeous in her red and gold dress, but she also wore a sad expression. I reassured her that I would be fine staying in with Mum, Dad and Gran. They wanted to cheer me up by playing board games such as *Monopoly* and *Cluedo*, but I preferred being alone in my room. I looked at my new outfit, hanging on the back of the bedroom door, threw myself on the bed and wept buckets. This was turning out to be a very merry mixed up kind of Christmas – one minute I'm feeling happy, the next down in the dumps. And I couldn't remember whose fault it was any more – mine, Angela or Bella?

# Chapter 10

# Strictly Sam and the Ballroom Dance Disaster!

You could be forgiven for thinking that my Christmas woes ended there. But there was still one more Christmas 'celebration' that could go wrong before Santa finally got to Summerlee on Christmas Eve: The Christmas Ballroom Dance Festivities.

Each year, the McKinneys held a Christmas Dance Competition plus Party. It was a very posh affair, with all of the dancers dressing up in proper ballroom costumes for the party and the competitive dances. There were lots of prizes to be won, but the most coveted had to be the McKinney Ballroom Dance Trophy for the most outstanding dance duo.

But this year's presentations were to be even more special. Apparently, the McKinneys had managed somehow to get Anton Du Beke – star of TV's popular dance show *Strictly Come Dancing* to come along and present the trophy.

Dennis Grant had won the trophy three years running with his partner Temara who had left him in the lurch by emigrating to Australia and now Dennis was stuck with me. We had only been dancing together for a matter of weeks, but he still expected to win the trophy. I don't know who was more excited about Anton Du Beke coming along – my Gran or Dennis Grant. They both think Anton is the best dancer since Fred Astaire (whoever he is).

No pressure on *me* then!

Mum and Gran were so thrilled at the thought of me winning the trophy with Dennis that they had a special ballroom dance dress made for me. Now, I'm sure Mum must have been thinking of her sticky out party frock days when she designed this, because that's what the dress was like – tangerine sequined bodice and zillions of voile petticoats complete with matching satin shoes and gloves. I looked like a giant tangerine spinning top.

Mum also created a special hair style – she stopped short of dying my hair bright orange but she managed to flatten my curls using wax gunge and then stuck a silly hair band onto the gloop. She did my make-up too, which was the least gaudy thing about me that evening. I took one look in the mirror and knew I would never have the nerve to play Saturday football ever again – I would be too busy being in permanent hiding. I suppose I should have been grateful that she didn't resort to using spray tan then I would really and truly have been *strictified!*

Nevertheless, my embarrassment was complete when I saw Dennis. He was wearing grey pin striped trousers, a white waistcoat and bow tie and a black tailcoat – the kind worn by his hero, Anton Du Beke on *Strictly*. Of course the McKinneys were thrilled that we had gone to so much effort to look the part. Me? I simply thought I had looked less conspicuous when I dressed up as my Gran!

The whole event was being held in the function room of a local hotel, to give us 'the feel of a real ballroom atmosphere', the McKinneys told us. The place was certainly busy enough – every relative and friend of every contestant had turned up in their Christmas-do finery. Mum and Dad, Gran, Rob and Angela occupied a table along with the Twins' parents. Dennis and his prim and proper parents and his even more prim and proper grandparents preferred to sit as close as possible to the McKinneys (and to Anton Du Beke) who were seated at the top table and as close as possible to the prizes and the *Trophy*. Dennis' eyes were glued greedily to the Trophy, as though at any moment some trophy burglar was going to burst into the room and steal it. The local press were out in force – all two of them – because of *the celebrity in the room*.

If I hadn't been involved in the dreaded competition, I could have been caught up in the jolly Christmas feel of the place. The function room was looking very festive: the walls were brightly decorated in gold, red and green ribbons and bows, with the most enormous Christmas tree I've ever seen, looking majestic at the front beside the stage. The tables themselves were very pretty: in the centre were decorative Christmas candles, surrounded by little plates of crisps, nuts and sweeties; there were also mini Christmas crackers and party poppers.

There was a proper band to accompany the dances, unlike the CDs which were used each week at the dance classes. We were told that we would feel like real dancers on the telly, dancing to proper live music. Live music or not, I doubt it would make me dance any better. I was beginning to feel really uncomfortable in my prickly frock. The waxy gunge was making my head itch and I spent most of the evening scratching it with my mum pulling my hands away and hissing in my ear, "Everyone will think you have an *infestation!*"

"Everyone will think I look like a *dork!*" I hissed in return. I couldn't wait for the evening to be over and get into my pj's. If only it was as simple as that. We had to 'enjoy' ourselves before *the real business of the evening* which was unfortunately hours away. There were novelty dances like *Grand Old Duke of York* and festive party games like *Musical Chairs* and *Pass the Parcel.* For a while, I did manage to have fun and forget that I looked like a pantomime dame or one of the ugly sisters from *Cinderella.*

Then came the announcement that the competition dances would commence and I just wanted to run to the toilets and be sick. Fortunately for me, the only prize Dennis was interested in was the big one – the trophy, so I didn't have to take part in any of the others. I was glad that the Twins, Debbie and Louise, won a prize for being the best newcomers. If only one of them had partnered Dennis, he might have a chance of holding on to his cup.

As the time of our competition dance drew closer, I became increasingly nervous. The butterflies in my tummy were doing battle with the numerous sweets I had consumed since we arrived and I felt distinctly unwell. I disappeared to the 'Ladies Powder Room' as it said on the entrance door to the most luxurious public loos I have ever been in. The toilet cubicles were reached by another door, but before that were the wash-hand basins – oval shaped glass with petal shaped soap dishes and scented rosebud soaps. Not for this place the yucky paper towels we had to suffer in school; instead proper cotton towels the size of facecloths – to be placed in a wicker basket after use.

I was so busy admiring the surroundings that I almost forgot about Dennis and the dance and got into a bit of a flap. I could hear Mum's voice hurrying me out of the cubicle before the cue for our first dance. At least, with all of the scurrying and dashing onto the dance floor, I had forgotten my nerves. There were only six couples in the final and there were three competitive dances which would contribute to the final score: quickstep, jive and waltz.

A frosty faced Dennis was already in the middle of the dance floor when I rushed on and into his arms. There was a loud gasp from the audience – my mother's choice of ballroom dance dress had made a big impact after all. The first dance was a quickstep, Dennis's favourite dance because of all the twirls around the room and quick changes of position. Before I knew it, Dennis was in full flight and I was being whizzed about the ballroom, feeling a breeze as we passed by a blurry crowd who were whistling and cheering and pointing at us. Dennis would be pleased – he liked to be the centre of attention, especially if the Judges' (and Anton's) eyes were drawn to us.

I was feeling quite relaxed by this time. I think the warm reception of the crowd had relaxed my nerves and I was able to follow the flow of the music. I was still feeling a bit dizzy with the spinning dance moves, and as I was passing our table, I glimpsed the rather horrified looks of Mum and Angela, with Gran in the background fanning her face with a napkin. The Twins were screeching their support, and the crowd was going mad. Even Mr Du Beke looked stunned.

Who needed Temara!

The music finally came to an end and I faced Dennis and curtsied as we had been taught. Now that I could focus more clearly and the band had stopped completely, I noticed that the applause was mixed with hoots of laughter and screeches from the Twins who came rushing towards me with what looked like a tablecloth and grabbed hold of me, pushing me in the direction of that luxurious loo. Dennis was still in mid bow and hadn't even noticed we had left the dance floor.

Once safely inside the Ladies' Powder Room, Debbie removed the table cloth, turned me round and pointed towards my reflection in the full length mirror. My jaw dropped to the floor.

*I had been whizzing round the dance floor with my voile petticoats tucked into the back of my knickers!*

And – unlike the telly show – they weren't matching the tangerine of my voile skirts. Nope – I had swapped those for a pair of red striped pyjama shorts because they kept the voile skirts from scratching my legs. I had hurriedly changed into them before the competition and that was why I was late onto the dance floor. Now, the whole of the Coatbridge dancing world and beyond would know my secret too. I couldn't bring myself to go back onto that floor and literally *face the music* and the hoots of laughter which would now surely follow me wherever I danced.

But, there were still two more competition dances left – the jive and the waltz.

I was rooted to the spot with fear. I started bubbling, using the tablecloth as a humongous hankie. I didn't want to let Dennis down, but my dancing was enough of an embarrassment without the further humiliation of having exposed my underwear – well my pyjamas – to the whole world! But, the show must go on – at least the Twins could go on in my place. There was nothing in the rules to say that a dancer couldn't *change* partners, so I sent Debbie and Louise out onto the dance floor: one would dance the jive and the other would partner Dennis in the waltz. Dennis would win his trophy and his reputation would be intact; my reputation would still be in tatters, but at least I wouldn't suffer the torture of having to dance again; everyone would get what they wanted – except for my poor Mum and Gran, who would have to stick with their dance idols on the *Strictly Come Dancing Christmas Special.*

And that's just what happened. Not only did Dennis win back his trophy, but he created a new record for winning a competition with the biggest number of partners. Anton Du Beke said he hadn't enjoyed a dancing competition so much in a long time. He said I reminded him of several of his partners form *Strictly* which seemed to tickle the funny bones of the older people in the room. Gran got over her *mortification* in time to have a *selfie* taken with Anton which, she said, would make her the envy of the women at the Thursday evening Crochet Club.

As for me, I was glad to get home and into my pyjamas for real. I think Mum learned the hard way that dancing wasn't going to be *my thing,* and said I didn't have to go back to the dance classes in the New Year. Dennis recruited the Twins as his new partners. He realised they were both talented dancers, with the added bonus that if one couldn't make a dance class, he would always have a partner in hand or *in hold*, as they say in the dance world.

# Chapter 11

# The Huge Hackit Hairy Spider at the Burns Brunch

Do you remember that I told you it had started to snow in December? Well, as it turned out, it snowed, and it snowed, and it snowed – right into the New Year.

Honestly, the news was full of kids all over the country, out on hillsides skiing or on sledges, and we, apart from a few respectable garden snowmen, were back at our desks on the dot of January 4th. Who would have thought that rusty old boiler would make it through the worst winter on record? Our school caretaker, Bill Watson, was proud of the fact that in the final year of the old building, he would have a perfect record of keeping the school open. I'm all for people getting their names into the *Guinness Book of Records*, but not when it prevents us kids from getting an extra week or two off school to enjoy the mountains of snow which had fallen on Coatbridge over the Christmas holiday.

After the Christmas Card Incident, I had made a New Year Resolution: Be kinder to Our Angela. On the last day of the Christmas term, Angela had organised a class party. She provided snacks and drinks and had made up little Christmas bags of sweets for each pupil. She played Christmas music and we danced and played party games. I'm sure that this was really for my benefit; she wanted in some way to make up for my disappointment at having missed the big party. We had collected enough money to give her flowers, chocolates and a cream woollen hat and scarf set which already came in a gift box. The Twins presented the chocolates and gift set and Paul Rankin bashfully handed over the flowers and dashed back to his seat to hoots and whistles from the rest of the boys. I could see how much the class loved Angela, and I knew that she was trying her hardest to be a good teacher. I decided then that I should at least give her a chance. And, the month of January was about to provide me with the ideal opportunity.

Angela wanted to devote some of our class time to the study of the poetry of Robert Burns, our famous Scottish poet. As soon as she mentioned the word *poetry* there was a unanimous moan from around the room. For some reason, children hate reading poems, but love writing them. But, Angela being Angela, this was to be a poetry unit with a difference. We would study the poetry and songs of Robert Burns, and something of his life story, with a view to having our own Burns Brunch – Angela's version of the Burns' Suppers which are traditionally held on or near his birth date, the 25th January. Angela was telling us that these Suppers were not only popular in Scotland, but all around the world, because our national poet's work was known and loved the world over.

Again, Angela had gone to a lot of trouble to make this learning experience different. She had permission to have our Burns' Brunch in the school cafeteria. Betty, the Manageress of the cafeteria, was going to put on Haggis and Neeps – the traditional Burns' Supper dish. Since we obviously wouldn't be drinking the traditional whisky, we could drink a small dram of Irn Bru, which was as popular as Robert Burns' poetry, but bad for our teeth, unless, as my future brother-in-law the dentist always says, we drank it through straws. We were very excited about the whole event – even Mrs McNulty hadn't done anything as adventurous as this.

We spent those first few weeks of term making posters and diagrams about the life and works of Robert Burns. Angela had started our study of one of his most famous poems, *Tam O' Shanter* by showing us a cartoon and then getting us to act out some of the scenes from this funny and spooky tale. We also read *To a Mouse*, and were asked to write serious or humorous poems about animals – in English or in Scottish dialect, if we preferred.

That lesson gave me a great idea for a humorous poem which I wanted to recite on the day of the Burns' Brunch. It would show Angela that I was really trying to be good and contribute to the class work in a more positive way. I also had a special surprise for the recitation, which I felt would make it really memorable. For the first time since August, I was really looking forward to school, and managed to forget that Angela was my sister and just concentrate on being a model pupil.

There was a lot to be done before the big day of the Burns' Brunch. Angela had made up a programme of who was doing what and in which order. The Twins were going to sing one of Rabble's most famous songs, *Red, Red Rose*, which really suited their sweet voices. I had locked myself in my room in the evenings, writing and rehearsing my funny animal – or should I say *beastie* – poem, careful that Angela wouldn't hear it until the day of the Burns' Brunch.

When the bard's birthday finally arrived, we spent the morning decorating the cafeteria with pictures of Robert Burns, and A3 posters of his poems. Betty had already set the tables, wrapping the cutlery in tartan napkins and putting a small display of plastic red roses in the centre of each table. The roses were, she said, because of the famous song *Red, Red Rose*. She wasn't sure if Robert Burns ever wore tartan, but she just wanted the place to look colourful. By midday, we were ready to begin.

One of our classmates, Calum Campbell, who was learning to play the bagpipes, did his best to pipe in the haggis, while we all stood at our tables and clapped in time to the music. Andrew Roberts read out the *Address to the Haggis* and then we sat down. Angela said the *Selkirk Grace* and that was the signal for us to 'tuck in'. But, it wasn't exactly burger and chips, and many of us had never tasted haggis before. Betty told us it was just like eating black pudding, so we gave it a try – mostly because we liked Betty and knew she had gone to a lot of trouble to make this event special. I have to say that it required a lot of Irn Bru to wash it down and keep it down. You would have thought we were being poisoned.

When we had finished eating, it was time for our versions of Burns' works or our original ideas inspired by his works. I could hardly concentrate for thinking of my performance and how my surprise would be received. Finally, it was my turn. Angela made the announcement that I was going to recite a poem I had composed myself, inspired by the classic *To a Mouse*. I tried to hide my nerves as I walked to the front of the cafeteria, where we were to perform. I knew people would be wondering why Dennis Grant, one of the quietest and brainiest boys in the class, (and my ex-ballroom dancing partner) was following me, clutching a large white shoebox. I heard Bella sniggering as he passed her table, "Oh, don't tell me it's a poem called *Wee sleekit, cowerin' timorous brain box* or *shoebox* added Danielle, proud of her contribution. Luckily, Dennis didn't hear them; he was so busy concentrating on keeping the box upright.

I had learned my poem by heart, so I didn't need any notes, and was free to give Dennis the signal to open the box. I took a deep breath and started:

"To A Huge Hackit Hairy Spider" by Samantha Winters

Huge, hackit, hairy sleekit spider,

Creepy crawlin' across the floor,

Where did yir ugly body spring from?

Wis it frae the windae or the door?


'But, dinna kill it, hen,'

Ma Daddy used tae say,

'Huge hackit hairy spiders,

They keep the beasties away.'

They mak thir webs all wiry,

Like silk threids hinging oot tae dry,

Beasties that create sic beauty

Dinna deserve tae die.'


I gave the signal to Dennis, who looked very serious as he opened the box to reveal a glass case, and scuttling about inside, the biggest, hairiest spider you've ever seen. I continued with the final verse, though having to raise my voice to compete with the admiring gasps of the boys and hysterical screeches of the girls:


*Still*, if I spy ye, hackit, hairy spider,

I wullna pick ye up, or pit ye oot,

Tae run and play wi'ither insects,

*I'll jist bluiter ye wi' ma boot!*


At the final line, a horrified looking Dennis sped off back to his seat in case I intended to act out the words. But he was so busy protecting the glass case containing his precious pet that he failed to notice Bella's leg sticking out from under her table ready to trip him up as he passed by. Dennis went flying and so did the glass box containing, Terry the Tarantula. As the box landed with a thump on a nearby table, the lid popped open and out tumbled the tarantula into the terrified crowd. Kids scattered to the four corners of the cafeteria, screaming for help, the police, their parents – anyone who would save them from the monster which had been let loose – however accidentally – from its glass cage.

My dream of putting on a spectacular performance had turned into a nightmare. Tables were overturned sending food and drinks flying. Angela, from her new position on top of one of the tables, was trying in vain to calm the pupils, but was angrily shouting for someone to kill the 'horrid creature'. Dennis, who was one of the few people in the room to remain calm, uttered that his pet 'was harmless' and 'since we were to be an eco school', 'murdering spiders should not be on our agenda'. (Sometimes, when Dennis spoke, he reminded me of Mr Bamber.)

Just at that, who should walk into the war zone, but the Head Teacher himself, followed closely by *Ms Snobby*. When he realised what the fuss was about, he turned whiter than snow; *Ms Snobby*, on the other hand, acted as though dealing with escaped tarantulas was part of the daily school routine. She quickly had us lining up and returning to our class. Mr Bamber seemed very keen to escort us, since Angela looked very upset and on the verge of tears. Dennis was left behind to find his spider and return it to its box and then home, when his parents could come to collect him.

In the afternoon, we were set to work quietly on our maths work; no reference had been made to the events of the morning. Angela was in control of the class, but very subdued. I'm sure she had been crying but had covered her tear-stained face with more make-up than usual. I sent a note of apology to Dennis, telling him I hadn't meant his spider any harm, and hoping that Terry was none the worse for his adventure. I left out the bit about Bella tripping him up – I would deal with Bella later.

That evening, we were all seated around the dining table, waiting for one of Gran's special treats. In she came and proudly passed round plates of – haggis and neeps!

"I got the idea from Angela's Burns' thingummyjig," she said. Dad tucked in, so did Mum, but Angela just took one look at the plate and rushed out of the room in floods of tears, with me following nobly to comfort her.

Well, two helpings of that rubbish in one day are too much for anyone – even a Burns' fan!

# Chapter 12

## Gran and the Sleepover-Makeover

Because of the trauma of the *spider incident,* Mum and Dad decided to treat Angela and Rob to a night out at a posh restaurant in Bothwell, a very posh place not far from Coatbridge. Dad promised jokingly that there would be no *haggis* on the menu which didn't raise a laugh but did result in one of Mum's *now don't you start your nonsense looks.* I didn't mind being left behind with Gran because my three best friends Holly, Debbie and Louise were coming to my house for a sleepover. Gran would settle down to watch her DVDs and we would be upstairs in my room watching our own collection of movies, playing our favourite music and tucking into more crisps, snacks and fizzy drinks than were good for us.

It promised to be a fun evening.

But, if you have ever been to a sleepover, you know that your best laid plans soon turn to boredom, and you get giggly and want something else to keep the giggles going.

"Let's go downstairs and ask your Gran to tell us some of her funny stories about the olden days," suggested Holly as she tucked into yet another chocolate.

"What a brill idea!" cried the Twins in one voice.

"I loved the one she told about her mother and her aunt washing blankets in the kitchen sink and getting into the sink themselves to trample the dirt out," said Holly.

"It must have been a shame to be without a washer dryer," sighed Debbie.

"Yes," said her sister, "but if they had, they would have missed out on all of that fun."

"Oh, all right," I said, "but if she is in the middle of a good film, we'll just leave her and come back upstairs." I loved Gran's stories too, but after all of the trouble I had been in recently, I wanted to keep in her good books.

We tiptoed downstairs and sneaked into the lounge. Sure enough Gran was stretched out on her favourite comfy chair, eyes closed, mouth gaping open to let out some hearty snores, oblivious to the strains of some scary songs being belted out opera style by Gran's heart throb, Nelson Eddy to his sweetheart; let's just say they would have gone out in the first round of *X-Factor*. My Grandpa used to say that if Gran fell asleep during a programme, it must be really good. If that was really true, what did she do during the really bad ones?

I was about to waken Gran when I spotted Mum's big make-up case in the corner of the room. She usually brings it in from the van at the end of the day, but she doesn't usually leave it out in the open like this. Like a mouse confronted by a huge piece of cheese, I just couldn't resist opening the box and showing off to my friends. I was going to sneak it upstairs to my bedroom, but when Gran was in a deep sleep, nothing could disturb her. I thought the girls and I could have some fun with Mum's make up and wigs and have everything put back before she came home or Gran woke up.

I did tell a bit of a fib though, when Holly asked if I was certain Mum would be ok with us using her stuff, and I said, "Yeah, sure! She lets me use it all the time." If Gran could have heard that, she would have been checking my tongue to see if it had turned black – 'a sure sign', she used to say 'that someone was telling lies'. (I didn't dare check my tongue in Mum's mirror – just in case.)

We took it in turns to give a makeover to one of the others. We pretended we were on the telly and were being timed to turn someone from an ugly duckling into a beautiful princess ready to meet Prince Charming at the ball. Then, Holly and I gave ourselves the task of trying to make identical twins, Debbie and Louise as different from each other as possible. We gave Debbie a long blond wig, and Louise a red curly wig; we made up Debbie in pastel shades to match her new blonde hair and gave Louise rosy red cheeks and lipstick to match. They certainly looked different from each other, but Louise burst into tears because Debbie looked pale and pretty while she looked like a model from the waxworks museum. After that, we got a bit bored with the whole game until Holly suggested that we give Gran a makeover while she was fast asleep, so that when she woke up and saw her 'new self' she would be over the moon.

At first I wasn't too keen on the idea. "But think of how happy she'll be," said Holly, "when she wakes up and sees the transformation."

In my head, I saw Gran looking like one of those glamorous film stars she so admired – so we set to work. Unfortunately, the picture I had in my imagination didn't transfer to Gran's face. We took turns at applying the make-up: Holly put on the foundation, but chose a bronze colour which made Gran look as though she had fallen asleep on the beach but had forgotten to stay in the shade; next Debbie attempted to tone down the bronze with some blusher, but somehow it emphasised the bronze even more and she looked like her face had caught fire; Louise had, as she thought, the simple task of applying Gran's ruby red lipstick, but her hands were trembling so much that most of the lipstick blended with the blusher on her cheeks resembling the war paint of some American Indian tribe. In fact, this whole new look which we were trying to create for Gran would be more likely to send her on the warpath rather than reward us for our efforts.

But, I had not given up hope of rescuing the disaster. I was sure that false eyelashes would make Gran so glamorous that she probably wouldn't notice the rest – unless, of course, she put on her spectacles. Now, I had watched Mum many times applying these lashes to her own eyes, but she would never let me have a go. As a result, when it came to transferring them to Gran's eyes without waking her, I lost my nerve, used too much glue and ended up sticking one eyelash to Gran's rosy cheek (which reminded me for a fleeting moment of Dennis Grant's pet tarantula) and the other attached itself to her hair which had already been the recipient of almost a can of *extra hold* hairspray. Gran snored loudly and we jumped back as if in time to some loud music.

We must have looked a pretty picture ourselves, and now we had turned my Gran into some kind of Frankenstein monster. My Gran hates horror movies. Now she looked as though she had just stepped out of one!

Gran stirred, yawned and stretched out her arms. She woke up, dozy for a few moments. She saw us standing in front of her just staring but saying nothing. We were too afraid to speak. Gran had wakened up before we had a chance to turn her back into a normal grandmother.

"Oh dear," she said. "My forty winks seem to have turned into four hundred winks. There, I've missed the end of that film again." We didn't make any comment.

"Cat got your tongue, girls? It's not like you four to be so quiet when you are together." I could hear Louise, who was right beside me, sniffling and her sniffles would turn into tears and then a confession. Then I would be in real trouble. Gran would probably have a heart attack when she saw how we had transformed her, I would be arrested for stealing Mum's property and my friends' parents would move away from Summerlee so that their daughters didn't have to associate with a known criminal. (I really must stop watching Gran's crime dramas, since I keep seeing myself as a villain – never a detective or a lawyer!)

Panic really set in when Gran fumbled around for her spectacles and made to get up out of the chair. "I've been neglecting you girls, so I'll just get up out of this lazy chair and make you some hot chocolate."

"Don't put yourself to any trouble," said Holly quickly. "We've stuffed our faces tonight, honestly and we're fuller than a wheelie bin."

"Yes," chorused the Twins, "not that we don't like your hot chocolate or anything like that."

Gran finally found her specs and put them on. We were still in the same position, too afraid to move yet dying to get upstairs to remove all of the gunge before Mum, Dad and Angela returned and I was accused of spoiling yet another night out. Gran finally got the specs on and peered out at us. We were taking tiny steps backward towards the door of the lounge.

"My goodness, Sam!" she said clearly shocked. "What have you done to yourselves? You're surely not thinking of going to one of those discos again, not at this time of night?"

"Don't be silly, Gran," I said, trying not to giggle at the strange sight of my Gran talking about our appearance when she hadn't a clue about our own. "We got bored watching DVDs and decided to play a makeover game." I knew at any moment she would catch sight of herself in the mirror above the fireplace – and she did!

Gran stared open-mouthed at her scary reflection, then at us, and then back at the mirror. Suddenly, she burst into laughter and it was infectious because we laughed too. If anyone could have seen the four of us roaring with laughter at our clown like reflections, they would have thought we had gone mad! Gran said through giggles, "Girls, that's the best laugh I have had in ages – better than a comedy. I look a dead ringer for Bette Davis in the classic film *Whatever Happened to Baby Jane.* (She later had to explain to us that this film was not in fact a comedy, but a kind of horror film. Bette Davis's character had been a child actress, the 'Baby Jane' in the title, who had gone a bit loopy in her old age and wore make up which made her look really scary.)

Eventually, we calmed down and Gran suggested that we all remove our make-up and sit down to steaming mugs of hot chocolate. As we sat around the fireplace, Gran suddenly looked sternly at us.

"There is one thing you must promise me, girls," she said in her most serious tone.

"Anything, Gran," I replied with the other three nodding furiously in agreement. "What is it?"

"Whatever you do," she went on with such a solemn frown, "do *not* take up careers in Hair and Beauty!"

# Chapter 13

## *Britain's Got Talent* at the School Parents' Evening

I'm not the kind of person who checks her horoscope regularly to see what life has in store. If I had, however, decided to look at what the Stars predicted for the month of February, I am sure it would have read as follows: *Neptune has collided with Mars to ensure a rocky start to this month which will lead to all-out war by the end of its short duration. Strained relationships with relatives may lead to rifts, and will certainly leave a nasty taste in your mouth.*

\*\*\*

February in class focused mainly on preparations for National Tests in English and Maths. Each day was spent on revision, until Angela felt that we were ready to take our tests. Each group was at a different level. I was much better at English than Maths, so I was looking forward to the three English papers, but dreading the two Maths' ones. Even our conversations during our interval and lunch breaks were taken up with *test talk* – especially since Angela was keen to remind us that our test results would be included in our forthcoming reports, *our last ever primary school reports.*

We were occupying our usual seats in the cafeteria one lunchtime when Holly suddenly exclaimed, "How weird is it going to be for your Angela to write a report on her own sister!"

"Perhaps she won't need to write it," suggested Paul as he paused from sipping his strawberry smoothie. "She can tell your mum and dad everything over the dinner table."

"That would be really cool," Andrew added, "because your parents don't even need to leave the house."

The Twins both exclaimed together, "I wonder what she'll say about you?"

Paul had a thoughtful look as he stirred his smoothie for the hundredth time. "I expect it'll all be good; she wouldn't want to say anything bad about her own sister, would she?"

Holly looked at me and said, "What do you think, Sam? After all it is *your* report and you're the only one who hasn't said anything."

That was just it – *I* didn't want to think about it *or* talk about it. How would Angela have room for all of the things which have gone wrong since August? Mrs McNulty's reports had always been full of praise, saying I had a 'vivid imagination and a flair for creative writing and drama'. Even when she commented on my lack of progress in numeracy, she made it sound like a compliment.

"I don't care about stupid reports," I finally said rather sharply, "especially not ones written by my big sister." Then I quickly changed the subject to football and asked Andrew and Paul if they wanted a kick about before the bell sounded for the end of lunch.

At home, Dad had started up his Old Dears' Tours for the new season, while Mum was busy rehearsing a Dolly Parton country and western song, hoping to wow Simon Cowell at the forthcoming Glasgow auditions for *Britain's Got Talent.* Between that and her busy appointments' book for her Beauty business, we saw even less of her than we did of Dad. I consoled myself with the thought that neither of them would be around to read the school report, so it was hardly worth Angela's time writing it anyway. Gran was delighted that her beloved *Countdown* was back on again, and when she wasn't glued to the television, she was trying out some new recipes she had seen on some cookery programme. (I secretly wished she would just stick to her own recipes which were much tastier.) And so, this haphazard house of ours led to my school report being read and mislaid in quick succession, resulting in neither of my parents noticing the time and date of the Parents' Evening.

Did I say *Parents' Evening?* In actual fact, it was Parents' *Afternoon,* because the whole event took place shortly after the school day ended. I think these meetings had taken place in the evening for so many years that it was difficult to change the title. Mind you, it was still getting dark fairly early, so I suppose the word 'evening' still applied, at least when the parents were coming out of the school. Dad was at the other end of Scotland, so it was left to Mum to come to the meeting. I was crossing my fingers and toes, hoping she would think it unnecessary, but Angela had other ideas.

"I think it would be unfair on Sam if the mums and dads of the other boys and girls see that her parents haven't turned up; they might think that's favouritism," she said, so Mum said she would check her appointments diary and make sure it was clear.

***

The day of the *Parents' Afternoon/Evening* finally arrived. We worked busily in the morning on a geography project, which was then displayed on the wall, alongside examples of our best work in story writing, art and history. We were very proud to see our work on the wall, and especially for our parents to admire. Angela had made sure that each person in the class had at least one piece of work on show. She was also very good at showing off the work to make it look even better than it was. She was a whizz with borders and multi-coloured frieze paper. And she made the headings for each section stand out beautifully because of her handwriting. Dare I say it again – even Mrs McNulty couldn't have produced a better display. But – I would *never dare* let Angela know I felt like this. I had made a New Year resolution to be kinder to her – but I still had a faint hope that she would move to another school before I went to high school.

At the end of the school day, Holly, the Twins and I, were asked if we wanted to stay behind and help serve tea and coffee to the parents while they waited for their appointments. We jumped at the chance to do what we felt was a very important job. We were instructed by *Ms Snobby* to report to Mrs Crangle in the Cafeteria and she would stock up our trays with a mix of tea, coffee and a plate of biscuits; we would each have our own supply of sugar and milk.

For ease, the actual meetings between parents and teachers were held at various points throughout the Cafeteria, which doubled as our Assembly Hall. Once the parents had spoken to the appropriate teacher, they were invited to go along to the classroom where senior pupils would be waiting to give them a guided tour. Dennis Grant, Andrew Roberts and Paul Rankin had been asked by Angela to supervise her own classroom. I think she wanted to make Dennis feel that there were no hard feelings over the spider incident – she had never quite recovered from the embarrassment of ordering the execution of the tarantula in front of the whole class *and* the Head Teacher. (Mind you, when I think back to his facial expression, I think Mr B. would have been the first person to congratulate the executioner.)

The place was beginning to fill up with parents, and we didn't have long to wait for our first 'customer'. I was paired up with Holly: one person to carry the tray and the other to hand over the tea and offer sugar and milk. I decided to be the tray bearer, since I thought that Holly had better *handing over the tea skills* as well as being sweet and polite (but not in a sickly way). I kept straining to see if Mum had arrived. I could just make out Paul's parents and Holly's mum, but no sign of my own. I was so busy after that, I didn't get a chance to look. Later, when the whole area was busy with parents and buzzing with chatter, I saw a sight which almost made me drop the tray in the lap of an unsuspecting parent.

My mum had arrived and what an entrance! This tear-stained, Dolly Parton look-alike was making her way towards Angela, who was in the middle of a serious discussion with Andrew's dad. Angela looked up, her mouth in mid-sentence. Mr Roberts looked up; in fact, it seemed as though the whole parent-teacher discussion had frozen in time, to take in the spectacle that was OUR MOTHER!

For once, my mortification and Angela's merged to become one HUMONGOUS moment of mortification.

Instinctively, I handed the tea tray to Holly and moved towards Mum to try and steer her back towards the door. But, she had already flopped down on the chair beside Mr Roberts and, black mascara rolling down her cheeks, launched into an account of her day at the auditions for *Britain's Got Talent.* Honestly, she probably didn't have a better, more interested audience in Glasgow than she had at that moment in our Assembly Hall.

"Oh, Angela!" she wailed, "I didn't even stand a chance. I had rehearsed my favourite song *Jolene* and I know if Simon Cowell had *just* got to hear me, he would have put me through to the next stage. Instead some young producer type was going along the queue holding out a clipboard like some kind of sword, pointing at some to stay and others to go because they 'didn't project the right image'. I mean, he looked as though he hadn't learned to tie his own shoelaces yet."

She paused only to draw breath and blow her nose, oblivious to the fact that a whole parents' meeting had come to a standstill and a crowd had now gathered round Angela's table to listen to Mum's tale of woe. I mean these parents – mostly women I have to say – were more interested in Mum's lack of progress at a talent show than the progress of their offspring during the most important year of their primary school education. Simon Cowell would have had the whole lot of them on his show if he had seen them! By this time, Angela had thrown her pen down and sat back, her hands covering her face.

But, Our Mum was in her element now as she battled through the tears with the next bit of her story. "I could see that I wasn't getting through to him, so I started singing right there in the queue. He walked right passed me as if he was deaf. I'm sure I have more talent in one false eyelash than he had in the whole of his clipboard." I could hear mutters of agreement from the crowd. One woman even put her arm around Mum and whispered, "There's always next year, love." Amazingly, Mum seemed comforted by these words, sniffed and dabbed her eyes with a muddy black handkerchief.

By this time, *Ms Snobby* had appeared, no doubt attracted by the crowd around Angela. "Is there a problem, Miss Winters?" she said, looking glad rather than really concerned. Then she caught sight of our mother, whose face was streaked with mascara. "Is there a problem with this lady?" She didn't even give Angela a chance to reply to the first question, before she bent over Mum. "Can I help you, Madam? Are you feeling unwell?"

*Ms Snobby* looked smug. It was as if she thought that Angela had upset a parent.

But, Angela saw the way that *Ms Snobby* was looking at Mum and she gritted her teeth as she spoke. "This is Mrs Winters, Ms Snodgrass, *Sam's* mother – and she is perfectly fine; she simply has a bad cold." Angela didn't shift her gaze from *Ms Snobby*, almost daring her to question Mum further. "My mother is simply overwhelmed at the *excellent* work Sam has achieved this year. She's just about to go home, when Sam has a moment to see her out." That was my cue to breeze past *Ms Snobby*, take Mum's arm and guide her to the door. The spectacle was over. The crowd went back to the mundane task of enquiring about their children's progress.

When Angela returned home that evening, however, she wasn't so sympathetic towards Mum. "Mum, how could you embarrass me like that? Imagine turning up in a stage costume and telling the whole world that you were auditioning for a TV talent show."

"Yes," Gran butted in, "it must have been really embarrassing, especially since you didn't get through." Trust Gran to 'get the wrong end of the stick' – yet one more of her own mad sayings.

"Oh, that's great," Mum said sarcastically, "I have two daughters, and not one of them appreciates the sacrifices I have made so that *their* dreams can come true, while mine have ended up in the wheelie bin." (I think that was a reference to the fact that she had chucked her Dolly Parton outfit in the bin as soon as she got home.)

Angela's face was as pink as her lipstick. (I hope she isn't going to start getting blotches, like *Ms Snobby*.) "My dreams have been shattered too, Mum. How am I going to face going back into that school again? I'll probably be asked to resign!"

*Resign!* Angela had said the magic word. And I couldn't be blamed, because it was all Mum's fault. I didn't hear the rest of the argument. I went off to my room to gloat over the fact that *my dream* had finally come true – Angela would be out of Summerlee Primary School within the month!

The next morning, I skipped merrily into the kitchen expecting to see Angela polishing off her resignation letter. She was there, looking her usual pristine self, all relaxed and composed.

"You look very cheerful for someone about to quit their job," I said, grabbing a slice of warm buttered toast and stuffing it into my mouth.

"That was last night," she said. "I've slept on it and realise that I was over reacting to the situation. It was my first Parents' Meeting and I was uptight. Besides which, Sam, Our Mum had every right to be there – *just not in that outfit*." Then she laughed, "It was worth it just to see the look of horror on Felicity Snodgrass's face. I think she thought Mum was drunk." I found myself laughing too. It didn't seem so at the time, but it was like a scene from a TV sitcom. Mum got to be a star of her own show after all!

The other thing that was funny – I should have been angry that Angela wasn't going to resign. But, I wasn't.

# Chapter 14

# Me and the Walk-On Walk-Off Part in 'Taggart'

Mum's disappointment over the *Britain's Got Talent* audition-that-never-was soon disappeared when she got a call from the Extras Casting Agency offering her another walk-on part in a TV movie of her favourite cop show *Taggart*. What's more, the scene involved a mother and daughter and Mum just happened to mention me and was told she could bring me along. I said, "Goody-goody!" when I heard, thinking I could take time off school and escape from Our Angela for a while. Then Mum informed me that filming would take place early on Saturday morning and would only last one day. One whole day – and a Saturday at that – for a teeny scene in a shop! I wondered how they ever got dramas made at all if it took so long!

It wasn't just that I was missing out on yet another Saturday, but Mum got me up in the middle of the night. At least it seemed that way – it was almost 6am and it was still dark outside. "Productions start early," she said as she poured milk over my cornflakes, "we have to be at Base by 7am as we have to be checked for costume and make up." I was about to remark that we were told to come in day wear and shouldn't need a costume check, but Mum told me to hurry up as we had to be on our way, since the production was being filmed on the other side of Glasgow.

Fortunately, Summerlee is not too far away from the M8 Motorway, and at that time on a Saturday morning the roads were virtually empty, so we were soon at our destination. I don't know what I expected – Hollywood glamour, big dressing rooms, huge studios? Not in Scotland. The 'studio' was a car park just off the motorway, where huge lorries were parked and lots of people were milling around, looking very cold and half asleep. One of the lorries doubled as a catering van, where the aroma of coffee and bacon wafted into the misty early morning air.

Mum informed me that most of these people were crew who would be first on site to get everything ready for the day's filming. They seemed to be queuing up for breakfast and heading into what could only be an old double-decker bus which had seen better days on the road. Mum dragged me over to the bus, informing me that this was a kind of waiting-room for the extras, but was also used as a kind of cafe where the extras and crew could eat their meals. She also told me that once we had been registered we would be able to get something from the catering truck too.

Once inside the bus, a young girl dressed in tatty combat jeans and a thick pullover, introduced herself as Fliss and crossed our names off a list clinging to an even tattier clipboard. (Throughout the day I would discover that the production team had stranger names than the actors: assorted shortened names such as *Cat, Jules, Josh* and *Jude* – perhaps everyday names like Jim and Jane were too ordinary for film and television careers?)

The bus wasn't very busy. We were informed by Fliss that we would be in two scenes: one taking place in a small newsagent's shop and the second when the detectives arrived on the scene. Mum said there would probably be quite a few extras playing the uniformed police, but they were probably in the costume truck getting into their proper police outfits. Another even younger girl wearing a knitted hat with ear flaps and multi-coloured fingerless gloves glanced at our clothes and said we would be ok. I thought she was going to send us to the make-up truck, where we might meet some of the stars of *Taggart* such as the chief detective, Burke or Jackie Reid, my mum's favourite character. But my mum, wishing to impress and already made up herself, offered to do my make-up and was given the go-ahead.

Eventually, we were allowed off the bus to get a drink and a snack. I don't usually like tea, but I felt that the bus was so cold I needed to be warmed up. While Mum was being served, I had a good look at my surroundings. It was daylight by this time and I could see just how crowded the car park was. There were some more extras dressed in police uniforms, looking so much like the real thing that I began to feel guilty as though I had committed a crime and they would, at any moment, grab me and put the handcuffs on.

I wandered away from the food truck to have a look at the other vans and hopefully find the star trailers which Mum had spotted on a previous job on the *Taggart* set. I kept looking furtively about me, in case the actors had bodyguards like the Royal Family had. The path between the trailers was empty so I took my chance, sneaking along and peeping at the names on the doors. I saw the name Alex Norton and below it his character name 'DCI Burke'. I could hear a deep voice coming from inside the trailer. It sounded very scary as though he was threatening someone. I hoped very much that he was learning his lines, because if he was just having a normal conversation, I wouldn't like to be the other person. (Mum told me that when he wasn't in character, he was very jolly and chatted away to the cast and crew.)

I moved away from the scary trailer to one at the end of the row. I spotted the character name first – DS Jackie Reid then her real name – Blythe Duff. I was so busy trying to work out how someone could get a strange name like *Blythe* when suddenly the door opened and out popped the actress herself. At first she looked startled, then her face crinkled into a smile.

"Hello. Are you lost, dear?" she said softly, just like her character in the programme. I was rooted to the spot.

There I was face to face with a famous Scottish actress and I couldn't utter a sound.

"You're my mum's greatest fan!" I eventually blurted out without thinking about the sense of what I was saying.

"Am I really?" she replied trying to suppress a smile. "Have I met your mum before? Is she an actress?"

"Yes, you have met her ... at least you don't know you have met her because she will have been in *Taggart* but not a big actress like you, just a little actress who is in a scene but doesn't really say very much, well she doesn't really say anything, but she thinks you're the bees' knees and can I get your autograph – for her, I mean – not for me – not that I don't like you or – anything?"

I stopped for breath, but I had babbled on so much like an idiot that I wasn't in the end really sure what I had said or what – if anything – Blythe Duff had understood. Just at that moment, DCI Burke's trailer door opened and he came out clutching what looked like a script.

"Are you ready, Blythe?" he said smiling. "Who's your little friend?" I was a bit miffed at the *little* reference. I am only eleven years old, but almost as tall as Mr Norton, even if he is an actor and famous and all that. (My Gran always says that the telly makes people look tall and it also makes them look fatter and older than they are in real life – and I think she has a point – except for the height thing.)

"I believe," said DS Reid, "this young lady is one of our background artistes. She and her mum must be in the newsagent robbery scene." No wonder she's a detective, I thought, working that one out when I hadn't even told her. Then I gave myself a row – mentally, of course – for mixing up fact with TV fiction. Again, I couldn't speak, or I preferred not to speak after my outburst to Blythe Duff, so I let myself be escorted back to the bus, walking timidly between DS Reid and DCI Burke, looking for all the world like a criminal being led into the police station. All I could think of was: what on earth is a 'background artiste' and why did my mum refer to us as 'extras'?

I was so lost in my own thoughts that I failed to notice the stern look directed at me by Fliss. "Please wait *inside* the bus until you are called," she said, but before I could utter any kind of explanation, Mum was already dragging me towards the bus and muttering in my ear.

"Samantha, I have never been so embarrassed. What on earth did you think you were doing talking to the actors? You could have us thrown off the set. We are not supposed to annoy the actors in case they are learning their lines. I should have known better than to bring you along." There was no point trying to talk to Mum when she was in a mood like that, no point trying to explain that I just wanted to get an autograph *for her*.

I thought it would be exciting, being on the set of a famous television programme, but between you and me – I thought it was rather boring. There was so much hanging around in the cold, draughty bus with nothing to do that I wondered why actors could be bothered. And, do you know what? They don't even film the story in its proper order. Mum and I were in a scene where we witnessed a robbery and the shopkeeper being attacked; then we were in a scene where we were interviewed by the police, *but* they filmed the police scene *first*. I mean, I had to act scared before I had even been in the scene where I get frightened in the first place. Mind you, I did get a word of praise from Alex Norton (DCI Burke), who said I was good at acting terrified. I didn't have the heart to tell him that I used being frightened of his scary voice from the trailer as my inspiration.

That word of praise from a famous actor also got me back in Mum's good books again, and she likes to embarrass me at every opportunity by boasting about it whenever she gets an audience of clients or aunties or anybody really who care to listen. You know, I couldn't have pleased her more if I *had* managed to get Blythe Duff's autograph.

# Chapter 15

## *Come Dine with My Mum* – a recipe for disaster!

If you thought that February couldn't get any worse for me – or for my mum – you were wrong.

As you will have gathered by now, my Grandma Winters is a fantastic cook. Her *tatties and mince* and her *stovies* – which is really tatties and mince cooked in the *same* pot – and her *homemade lentil* soup are legendary; and my mum – well let's just say that she was absent when they were doing cookery lessons at school. Dad once bought her one of those *Spend a day with a Celebrity Chef* vouchers for Valentine's Day. Well, apart from the fact she thought it was the most unromantic present ever, she almost burned down the Celebrity Chef's brand new Edinburgh restaurant. Burning food is something she's *very* good at.

My gran, who always said that she was too young to sign up to one of Dad's *Old Dears' Tours* changed her mind when he told her that he was taking a trip to the Western Isles, and in particular, Barra. Gran said she had always wanted to visit that island because when she was younger she had written to a girl there. The 'girl', who, like Gran would be almost eighty, had emigrated to Canada many years ago, but Gran had as she called it a 'hankering' to visit the place anyway. Now, we were all delighted that Gran was finally going to have a break, because she hardly ever wanted to go away from Summerlee, but then it dawned on me – Mum would be in charge of cooking. Gran offered to cook some of her classic dishes and put them in the freezer, but Mum insisted that *her* cooking had come a long way from the time when she had the disaster at the Celebrity Chef weekend Dad had once bought her as a present.

When she says it had improved, what she *really* meant was that she had been watching every episode of *Come Dine With Me* and *Masterchef* plus celebrity versions of both programmes. Personally, I think the jungle food in *I'm a Celebrity, Get Me Out of Here.* looks cordon bleu compared to Mum's burnt offerings.

Mum's determination to cook was sealed when Gran gave her a lecture on how things were in her young day: 'Girls learned by watching their mothers cooking and baking and got their cookery skills by imitating them. When we were at the Big School' (Granspeak for High School) 'we all took classes in Domestic Science' (Granspeak for Home Economics) 'and we learned how to sew. Schools should go back to basics!'

So it was that Angela and I (and sometimes Rob) were subjected to a week of indigestion and starvation while Mum tried out a series of exotic dishes while we were longing for a plate of Gran's stovies. Rob even offered to take us out for dinner one evening, but Mum said, "Not at all, Rob, you and Angela are saving for a wedding. Besides which, there is nothing better than coming home to a home-cooked meal, is there?"

Poor Mum! She did her best, even rearranging her clients that week so that she could spend more time in the kitchen. But, you couldn't exactly label her food *comfort eating!* And why is it that the telly kitchens always look immaculate no matter how many ingredients or pots and pans are used? Mum's kitchen always ended up looking like a rubbish tip, and a good candidate for one of Gran's other favourite programmes – *How Clean is Your House?* And all of her efforts resulted in a few inedible morsels which wouldn't feed a budgie. (Trust me when I say a budgie wouldn't even peck at it anyway.)

I became so desperate that I composed a letter of complaint to the Scottish Parliament, demanding that they ban all cooking programmes from the telly and send all mums to cookery schools staffed by grandmothers who know how to conjure up home-made soup and stovies. Furthermore, I pointed out that if they did not take immediate action, they would be responsible for the huge numbers of children who were flocking to fast food restaurants. (Notice that I did *not* make any demands for them to close all fast food restaurants.)

At the end of a long, hungry week, I was ready to eat the furniture and was really looking forward to Gran's return. Then came the phone call. It was Dad on his mobile from the isle of Barra when he should have been on his way home to Summerlee.

"Sorry, Sam but there's been a bit of a problem. We're not going to make it back on Friday after all. Our ferry is stuck on South Uist and can't get across to Barra to pick us up. One of the locals has told us that it can sometimes be stuck for several days, even weeks. But, Sam, tell your Mum not to worry – the food here is fantastic. *At least we won't starve!"*

# Chapter 16

## The Not So Great Outdoors...

Now, Our Angela loves all of the stuff we do inside the classroom, even the boring stuff like maths and science projects, but when it comes to the physical stuff like PE or working outside in the eco garden it's obvious that she is completely 'out of her comfort zone', as I've heard people say on the telly.

She, as Gran would say, 'puts a brave face on it', but apart from choosing trendy gardening gloves and boots, or sporting an up to the minute track suit, she really doesn't have a clue. My classmates wouldn't really notice such details; they still think Angela is heavenly, but I do and I'm sure Bella has picked up on it. Bella, however, had been on her best behaviour because she knew that the weekend trip to the Auchterallan Outdoor Centre was coming up, and she didn't want to be excluded from all of that freedom to cause as much mischief as she could cram into a few days. She hadn't said as much, but I knew the way Bella's mind worked, and I knew that she was even less of an outdoors person than my sister.

***

It was only a weekend trip – leaving school on the Friday morning and returning on the Monday afternoon – but Angela saw it as a *lifetime* away from Rob and her home comforts. A Mediterranean Cruise, full of fine food and three outfits per day – that's our Angela. She's not vain, but when she does go on a trip it's a suitcase for the clothes, one for the shoes and matching handbags and one for the make-up and accessories. So, I wasn't surprised when I overheard her moaning to Mum about a weekend miles away from any kind of luxury.

"I tried to get out of it. I offered to take extra classes, anything but go on this trip to the middle of nowhere, but Felicity Snodgrass insisted it would look good on my report and that it would let the pupils see me in a different light. Huh! I think she knows I can't stand the thought of creepy-crawlies and likes the thought of me falling flat on my face – *literally*."

"You're so good at everything," said Mum reassuringly. "I'm sure you'll be wonderful at coping with the outdoors."

"I just wish I had your confidence. I know that Sam is going to hate me being around. She'll probably think I'll cramp her style. I hope Dennis Grant doesn't bring his pet tarantula!" she sighed as she went upstairs to try and cram her luggage into one holdall and spend endless hours on the phone saying tearful goodbyes to Rob. I had already packed and was relaxing on my bed, having zoomed up the stairs two at a time before Angela realised I had been ear-wigging.

On the morning of our trip, Angela and I set off together in Rob's car for the short journey to the school. It was still cold and frosty, but luckily no snow. The sun was even making the effort to shine, however feebly. Mum and Gran both hugged us and waved us off from the front door. Fridays were very busy for Mum's Beauty business and she had to make an early start. Gran had wanted to wave us off from the school, and Rob had offered to take her there and back in the car, but her arthritis was playing up and she thought it best to remain indoors. "Have a good weekend, girls," she shouted as we got into Rob's car. 'Girls', she had said, as if we were both school kids and Angela wasn't a grown up, never mind a teacher.

The coach which was to transport us to Auchterallan Outdoor Centre was already parked outside the school gates, and a group of excited classmates stood chatting as they waited for the signal to get on board. I got out of the car, grabbed my back pack and headed for Holly and the Twins who were trying to avoid being hit by the football which Paul and Andrew were messing about with. I wanted to join in the kick about, but I thought it best to save my energies for the weekend ahead.

Mr Bamber appeared clutching a clipboard and looking rather bizarre in his casual costume. We were so used to seeing him in smart suits, shirts and ties that the sight of him in denim jeans, an open necked check shirt, hiking boots and wax jacket took us by surprise. He looked like an overgrown boy scout. When the silver haired driver of the coach spotted the Head Teacher, he folded up his newspaper, tucked it into his jacket pocket, and climbed down the steps of the coach to see to our luggage. (For a moment, I thought of Dad and whether he was doing something similar on his coach – though *his* passengers would be as silver haired as our driver, and probably not shrieking with excitement.)

Once Angela had waved goodbye to Rob, she quickly came over and got us into a line so that Mr Bamber could check names on his clipboard list.

Everyone was present – except for Bella, Jade and Danielle. We shouldn't really have been surprised – they wandered into school several minutes after the bell, morning and afternoon, and no amount of notes to parents or detention for the three offenders improved their timekeeping. As my Gran would say, 'those three girls would be late for their own funerals'.

Mr Bamber ushered us into our seats, and by the time we were all settled with our seatbelts securely fastened and the driver had started up the engine to heat up the coach, we saw three bedraggled figures with red faces huffing and puffing their way towards the coach. With no apologies to Angela or Mr Bamber, the latecomers dumped their luggage at the side of the bus and clambered up the stairs. They said no hellos to any of us, but made their way directly to the back seat, ignoring the fact that there were plenty of empty seats towards the middle of the coach. It was a huge coach for such a small group, but we did have a lot of luggage, and I'd heard Angela say that Mr Bamber would be bringing along supplies of bottled water and juice, plus some treats – but she didn't know exactly what these *treats* would be.

Suddenly, we were on our way, waving excitedly to the parents and guardians who had managed to come and see us off, some few dabbing their eyes with hankies; others were shouting, 'Have a good time' or 'Be good' or both. The waving seemed to carry on until we had moved out of the town itself, but we were happy to wave to shoppers or pedestrians or anyone who looked towards the coach at all. Eventually, we calmed down and occupied ourselves with chatting, reading, playing with iPods or simply looking out of the window.

At one point, Bella's voice belted out the song: 'The front of the bus, they cannae sing, they cannae sing, they cannae sing'. She nudged her companions, Jade and Danielle to join in, which they did – tunelessly. A few of the boys at the front responded with the expected: 'The back of the bus they cannae sing, they cannae sing, they cannae sing, the back of the bus they cannae sing, they cannae sing for peanuts'. Bella resumed her verse but accompanied it by firing peanuts in the direction of the singers in the front of the bus. But, several of the peanuts caught Mr Bamber in the neck. The singing was swiftly banned and Bella's peanuts confiscated.

We were allowed to eat snacks or drink juice, but we had to put our empty papers or bottles into the bags which the driver had attached to the side of each aisle seat. We were forbidden to have our mobile phones with us. Most people in our class hadn't been away overnight without our parents before, but if we did get homesick, Mr Bamber and Angela both had mobile phones and a list of contact numbers for each pupil's family. Of course, I was teased about *not* being homesick because my big sister was on the trip, but I retorted that Angela was more likely to get homesick for her fiancé than I would for our parents. (Not because I wouldn't miss them, of course, but I felt quite grown up.)

We were heading north, but since geography was never a strong point or an interest of mine, I didn't really remember much else about the route we were taking. There was a microphone at the front of the bus for the use of the driver, but Mr Bamber was in his element every few miles, by informing us of places of interest, except that the only person who was really interested was Dennis Grant, whom we sometimes called *Dennis Google, the human search engine* because of the things he stored in his mind. But he usually ended up correcting

Mr Bamber's incorrect facts. I vaguely remember mention of Stirling and then Perth, and then I was too busy chatting to Holly until Mr Bamber announced that we were approaching our destination.

I hadn't noticed when we had last driven past a town or a village. Now we were crawling along a narrow strip of country road, hardly wide enough for a van, let alone a huge coach. It was like the yellow brick road from the film – it seemed to lead to nowhere but at the end of it lay something that everyone couldn't wait to see – Auchterallan Outdoors Centre.

Clouds sailed across a blue sky, masking the pale sunlight. There was still evidence of the dreadful winter in the fields where the grass struggled to rise above the grey blankets of snow. We continued along the bumpy road till we came to a clearing and the coach drew to a halt in a huge parking area of red stones which made a crunching sound as the bus reversed into a parking bay reserved for coaches. Mr Bamber was quick to order us to remain in our seats until the driver had a chance to unload our luggage, but we were too fidgety to stay seated for long – we wanted to see where we would be lodging for the next three nights.

Finally, we trooped off the bus and had a better chance to take in our immediate surroundings. There were two buildings: our accommodation was a huge wooden chalet, like the kind you see in pictures of Austria or Switzerland, except not so pretty or colourful. Opposite stood a barn-like building which housed a shop plus storage facilities for additional equipment we might require for our outdoor activities. The buildings were surrounded by woodland, and snowy topped hills stretching up behind the main chalet. Once the bus had been emptied, we were surprised to see the driver hop in and drive off back down the rocky road to civilisation; he wouldn't be needed during our stay, so he would return for us again on Monday afternoon. We were almost in tears, as though we were being abandoned on the set of a spooky film, stranded until our rescue by our silver haired coach driver in a few days' time.

That feeling didn't last long once we were escorted inside by Gregor and Cathy, our instructors for the weekend. We were desperate to see our rooms and unpack our stuff, so that we could explore our surroundings before teatime. Because we were the only group booked in for that weekend, we were allowed two or three to a room instead of the usual four. The boys, along with Gregor and Mr Bamber, would occupy the rooms on the first floor, with Cathy, Angela and the girls on the second floor, in attic type rooms with sloping ceilings. I shared with Holly and we were delighted that our room was next door to Debbie and Louise. We were also glad that Bella, Jade and Danielle were at the opposite end of the corridor, next door to Angela and Cathy. There were toilets and shower rooms at both ends of the corridor, but I'm sure Angela was relieved to find en-suite facilities in the staff quarters, though pretty basic – no fluffy towels or toiletries provided here.

From the windows in our room, we could look out onto the hills at the back of the building. Somewhere in the distance were the river and the famous gorge which we had heard so much about and which filled us with dread because of the (no doubt exaggerated) tales which had been passed onto us by former pupils from our school. Down through the years, it had become the most favourite *and* the most feared of the activities at Auchterallan Outdoor Centre.

We were starving by the time five o'clock arrived and we could head downstairs to the restaurant which was situated on the ground floor across from a recreation room. Imagine our surprise and whoops of delight when we saw that fish and chips were on the menu, as well as tuna pasta bake – or macaroni cheese if you were a vegetarian. (There were no vegetarians in our class, but some people opted for that anyway.) I'm rather fond of macaroni cheese myself, but only when I don't have the option of fish and chips. We weren't allowed fizzy drinks with our meals – we could choose from ice cold milk, water or diluted fruit juices. For pudding, it was yoghurt or fresh fruit. I suppose we had to make *some* sacrifices for the fish and chips. Besides which, we were allowed cans and sweets later after our first activity. I thought we would be relaxing on that first evening, but we were quickly reminded by Gregor and Cathy that this was an *activity weekend*.

As soon as it was dusk, we were herded over to the supplies building where we were kitted out with wellies and balaclavas – even us girls. Angela's face fell as soon as she saw the assault course which we would be attempting. Climbing ropes and crawling through muddy pipes filled us with excitement, but Angela looked as though she was about to faint. I could see the relief flooding her face when Cathy informed her and Mr Bamber that they would need to follow the boys and girls and supervise, while Gregor and Cathy 'showed us the ropes'. Even outdoor instructors have their own funny sayings. (Some day, I shall write a book entitled *The World is Full of Funny Sayings*. In fact, I probably have enough to fill one volume at the moment.) Angela's first task was to run and find Bella, who had disappeared after tea and hadn't changed into her warm outdoor gear. She looked very sullen as she joined her two pals, and kept whispering to them when she was supposed to be following Cathy's instructions and demonstration of the most effective way to tackle the 'tunnel' as the pipe was called.

Cathy and Gregor divided us into groups, with each group working on a different section of the assault course, but by the end we would all have completed the tunnel, the rope ladders, running over log hurdles and moving across a fast flowing burn by holding onto a thick rope tied to two trees at either side of the burn. That was my favourite part. Our team was just pipped at the post by Paul Rankin's. Bella's team was last because Jade got stuck in the tunnel while Danielle refused to cross the burn on a 'stupid old rope that looked as though it was about to snap'. I didn't mind; it meant we got first shot at the showers and straight into our pj's. These instructors are very crafty; what with the long journey and the assault course, we were too exhausted to have a carry on or sit chatting into the night. I think we were all fast asleep before nine o'clock. Now that is a record! We didn't even have any supper or the snacks which we had sneaked into our hold-alls. It also meant that Holly didn't notice that some of her sweets and cans were missing from her locker beside the bunk beds.

Imagine having to get up on a Saturday morning at the same time as a normal school day. I certainly missed our central heating. Our attic room which was quite large and airy only had storage heaters, so the room tended to get chilly quickly when the heaters were off. I had put several pairs of sock slippers on and was relieved I had packed my woolly pyjamas which Gran gave me at Christmas (actually she bought me the same type of pyjamas *every* Christmas). Holly, who was even sleepier than I was, kept diving under the duvet, reluctant to leave the bed which was warm and cosy compared to the rest of the room.

Eventually we made our way down to breakfast. The Twins were already seated; Louise was looking glum and Debbie was trying to cheer her up as Holly and I sat down beside them.

"What's up with you two?" I asked, pouring milk over my cornflakes.

"Louise has lost her silver locket," whispered Debbie somehow anxious that no one should be able to eavesdrop. I could understand that, since the adjacent table was now occupied by Bella and her cronies. We all knew how special the lockets were to the Twins, because they had been sent to them from their godmother in America. Debbie continued. "She definitely had it when we arrived, because I saw her put it into her little velvet jewellery pouch before we went on the assault course yesterday evening."

Louise finally spoke while bravely trying to fight back tears, "I know I put it there, but when we got into our room last night, the pouch was lying on the floor beside the bed. Surely it hasn't been *stolen*?" At that word, I found myself looking over at Bella's table. There had been occasions in our class where stuff had gone missing, mostly pencils or pens, but sometimes money. I always wondered if it had been Bella because nothing like that had ever happened before she arrived in our class. We *all* suspected Bella; I'm sure Mrs McNulty did too, but Bella always had an excuse for her whereabouts or a solid alibi provided by Jade or Danielle or both. My eyes must have glazed over because the next thing I realised was Bella making a funny face and muttering, "Want your eyes back!" I turned away quickly, thinking that if Bella could have read my mind at that moment, she would have jumped over the table to *scratch my eyes out.*

Always the practical one, Holly said, "Have you checked under the bed and in between the duvet and the sheets? We were all so exhausted last night that we didn't know what we were doing."

"Yes," sighed Louise. "We stayed up for ages emptying our entire luggage onto the beds, searching in cupboards and drawers which we hadn't even used. I kept expecting Miss Winters to come in and tell us off for not having the lights off."

"What about your locket?" I asked Debbie. She pulled the locket out from the collar of her polo shirt, almost ashamed to show it because it would remind her twin of her own loss. "It'll turn up," I said in the most reassuring voice I could muster. "We'll let Angela know." (I couldn't call my sister *Miss Winters* unless we were actually inside our school building. It still seemed strange to say it or hear it at all.)

We had to leave it there, as Mr Bamber had summoned everyone into the recreational room where Gregor and Cathy would outline the day's programme. They informed us that our morning activity would be rock climbing at the gorge. It involved working with a partner and was a great exercise in trust as well as physical skill. I was really excited at the prospect of climbing, or indeed any of the physical activities since I loved being outdoors. I glanced at Angela standing beside Mr Bamber and trying to look enthusiastic. I realised that here, she would be less likely to enjoy the admiration and adulation of my classmates. Angela would be trying her hardest to blend into the background, and this would give me a chance to shine.

It suddenly dawned on me that this was how I saw Angela – a *rival* for the esteem of my friends and classmates. I had been competing with her since August, and up until now, she had been winning. But, Auchterallan was *my* kind of place and Angela was like a fish out of water. For the first time in my life, I felt superior to my sister – and I liked the feeling!

I was so lost in thought that I almost missed Cathy telling us about our choice of afternoon activities which included canoeing, swimming or hiking. Then, we would have some free time to relax and wander about, or in the boys' case, play some football. We would round off the day by having a games night in the recreation room with prizes and the treats which Mr Bamber had been so secretive about on the way here. That was the good news. The bad news – well, to 'take us out of our comfort zone', Gregor had put our names into a hat, and we would be partnered with the person whose name was drawn out after our own. I was disappointed that Holly and I were unlikely to be working together. She, in fact, was partnered with Louise; Debbie with Dennis; Andrew with Jade; Danielle with Paul; and me – with Bella. I was glad she hadn't got one of the twins or Holly, because of her past record of bullying them, but I just wish it had been one of the boys, and not her.

# Chapter 17

# Climb Every Mountain...

Kitted out with safety helmets and harnesses, climbing boots and gloves, we followed Gregor and Cathy down to the gorge, chattering excitedly as we trundled over rocky paths and mud puddles until we reached our destination. Angela and Mr Bamber followed at the end of our group to make sure there were no stragglers. The sun was flitting in and out of the clouds, as though involved in a game of heavenly hide and seek. The clouds, I am glad to say, didn't appear threatening being all white and fluffy, so we were confident that our rock climbing wouldn't be interrupted by rain. We soon came upon the natural, rugged rocks which constituted the infamous gorge. It looked very imposing, and to us high as a mountain, though most of us had never seen a mountain let alone stood next to one. Gushing down the right-hand side of the gorge was a fast flowing waterfall which merged with the burn we had crossed the previous evening.

We gathered round in a semi-circle to watch Gregor and Mr Bamber demonstrate how we would negotiate our climb. Cathy and Angela would stay at the bottom to help us secure our equipment and get a solid foothold on the rock. Once at the top, Mr Bamber and Gregor would remove the safety harness and direct us down the path which led back to the Centre. I have to say that our Head

Teacher's street cred climbed higher than a mountain that day, when we saw how easily he negotiated the climb, without once slipping or trying to outdo the more experienced climber, Gregor. Of course, Mr Bamber had been coming to the Centre for hundreds of years, and had probably done this climb lots of times – but we were seeing it for the first time, and he looked pretty cool to us just then.

Bella seemed very keen to go first. Trust her to want to show off, but I wasn't going to let her think I was scared – which I wasn't anyway – so, off we went. Cathy told us to take our time, suggesting that Bella and I would take it in turns to get a foothold in the rock, with the partner supporting until it was her turn. I was told to move off first, and I don't think Bella liked that because she hissed into my ear, 'teacher's pet', but I just ignored her and got started. Angela tried not to look scared for me and managed a cheerful 'Good luck, girls' and we were off!

We started slowly and carefully. Cathy was shouting positive comments from below, but telling us not to look down, especially as we clambered further up the rock face. Then Bella got impatient. "Snails could go faster than you. *Sammy Snail*, we'll be calling you after this," she taunted.

"I'm following instructions, Bella," I snapped back, trying to keep my balance as Bella was tightening the rope deliberately. "That way we'll get to the top in one piece." But this made Bella more determined to outdo me. When it was her turn to take a few steps, she managed to lean over and kick me in the shins, so that I lost my footing. I yelped with pain, but Bella had been clever. We were too far from the ground for anyone to pinpoint what was going on, and too far in for Gregor or

Mr Bamber to spot anything as they looked downwards. I wanted to kick back, but much as I hated Bella at that moment, I knew that safety was the most important thing while we were so high up.

I checked Bella's progress till I could steady myself and get my foothold again. We were inching closer to the top, and I could hear the voices of Mr B and Gregor, encouraging us. I took a deep breath, loosened the rope and let Bella move ahead, but taking care that she couldn't repeat her previous effort to topple me. She didn't try any more tricks and we were soon being hauled onto safe ground by Gregor who congratulated us on our 'excellent team work'. As soon as her harness was unfastened, Bella belted down the hillside path as though her life depended on it. I assumed she was avoiding facing me after almost causing a fall, but I held on for a few minutes to catch my breath and wait for the next pair to arrive.

It was Holly and Louise, looking very pleased with themselves. I was glad that the climb seemed to have taken Louise's mind off her missing locket. Louise wanted to wait at the top for her twin to arrive, so Holly and I decided to saunter down to our room and chill out till lunchtime. As we made our way upstairs, we passed a sheepish-looking Bella stuffing something into her pocket. She brushed past us without as much as a hello or excuse me.

"She's looking guilty about something," Holly said.

"Bella always looks guilty about something and she usually *is* guilty," I said, and I told her about the incident on the rock face.

"You could have been killed, Sam," she said. "Why didn't you tell Mr Bamber?"

"Because no one could have seen anything. She was clever enough to wait till we were at least half way into our climb," I said. "But, I don't think that's the only thing she's guilty of. I'm sure she's stolen Louise's locket."

"You know, Sam, I think you're right," Holly said, chewing her lip. (She always did that when she was thinking something over.) "I thought I was missing some cans and sweets, and I knew you wouldn't take anything without asking first. Perhaps Bella has been stealing more than jewellery. Let's sneak into her room while she's out and see if we can find anything." I was tempted to go along with this suggestion, but it would be too risky if she suddenly came back, and knowing Bella, she would somehow turn the accusations on us. I managed to persuade Holly that we should wait and just keep a closer eye on her, make sure she didn't get another chance to rummage about in other people's rooms.

It was too much of a coincidence that Bella's turning up last to everything coincided with missing food and jewellery. Now I knew why she had been so keen to come on this trip.

By this time, the others were trickling in for lunch which consisted of sandwiches, juice and a piece of fruit. We warned the others about our suspicions, and to be careful of leaving stuff lying about. As it turned out, Andrew thought that a £5 note had been taken from his wallet, but he couldn't be sure that he hadn't dropped it somewhere. We wondered how many other people in our group were missing stuff which they hadn't yet discovered. We tried to change the subject to something more pleasant, like which activities we had opted for in the afternoon.

The afternoon passed uneventfully. The sun kept shining for us and we made the most of it with our various outdoor pursuits. I went canoeing with Holly, Andrew and Paul, while the Twins and Dennis opted for swimming in the Centre's outdoor pool. The groups which hadn't opted for these pursuits went hiking with Mr Bamber and Angela. Gregor and Cathy were needed to supervise our groups, so Mr Bamber was in charge of the hiking, with Angela along as unwilling helper. I could see that she still wasn't enjoying herself, and I had noticed that she was unusually sharp with Bella, Jade and Danielle, who had turned up without the proper hiking gear and were sent back to change, thus wasting precious time. But, I did notice that Angela had made a point of going back into the chalet with them. I wondered if she too suspected them of being up to no good.

I enjoyed the canoeing experience. Gregor was a good instructor and I felt proud that I had learned a new skill. It was back to our rooms to get showered and changed and then we had some free time before our tea time meal which was to be an hour later than usual. When we had finished eating, we would go straight into the recreation room to play games or watch TV until it was time for the Games' Tournament to begin.

Holly and I had arranged to meet the Twins outside and we would go for a walk and chat about our favourite bits so far. I went downstairs first; Holly had permission to phone her parents, so I said I would wait outside. I expected that the Twins would be waiting for me because I thought I had heard their voices on the landing outside our room while I was getting dressed. But, there was no one there. I hung around, enjoying the peace and quiet, and wishing Summerlee could be as sunny as this place. Suddenly, I heard a piercing scream, coming from

145

the area of the gorge. I thought at first it must be someone larking about or playing Hide and Seek. Then I heard it again, this time louder and more urgent.

I ran as fast as I could in the direction of the scream, which did lead me, tripping and stumbling, towards the gorge, where we had completed our rock climbing task that morning. I couldn't believe my eyes – what I saw was like something out of a movie.

Debbie was held kicking and screaming by Jade and Danielle, who had her pinned against a tree. Bella was laughing and shouting orders to someone, but I couldn't make out who it was until I got closer.

"That'll teach you to accuse me of being a stealy-thief, Misses High and Mighty Twins. Now, climb, you wimp!" Then Bella's voice became even more menacing. "Climb or I'll order Danielle and Jade to give your sister a real doing!" The voice which answered feebly was one I recognised – it was *Louise* and she was perched on the footholds of the gorge, almost a quarter of the way up, but without any protective head gear or safety harness!

I was jolted into action. I rushed towards Bella and let out a roar as I threw myself on top of her, forcing her to the ground. I wasn't sure what I was going to do once I had knocked Bella to the ground. Remember I told you that I'm not really a fighter, but Bella has had loads of experience, as I soon found out. She was pulling at my hair and digging her nails into my face as we rolled about on the grass and pebbles, heading down towards the waterfall. I shouted to Debbie to get loose and go for help, but was soon muffled by Bella's hand clamped over my mouth. I could hear Louise wailing that she was losing her grip, and I was determined to make a break for it and help her down.

I did manage to wrestle free and was crawling towards the rock face when I felt something grip my two ankles. Bella was dragging me backwards, and calling to her cronies to come and help her. I think she meant one of them to keep hold of Debbie, but the two girls were so used to obeying Bella's commands immediately that they both left their posts, allowing Debbie to run off and fetch some adults. Every bone in my body was aching and I could feel sharp twigs and branches cutting into my skin, but I didn't give in. Now, I was being pinned down by Jade and Danielle while Bella went over to where Louise was precariously perched.

"Don't you think we should make a run for it, Bella?" pleaded Jade while sitting on my legs. "We're in real trouble if we're caught here."

There was no hint of fear in Bella's voice when she replied, "We might as well finish what we came to do then." I managed to bite Danielle's hand which was covering my mouth, and I held my head up as far as I could in time to see Bella climbing deftly up the rocks. I could guess what she was about to do – she was going to kick Louise's foot away from the rock, just as she did to me, making sure that Louise would lose her grip altogether and fall to the ground.

I knew that Bella was tough, but I never thought for a moment that she could be so vindictive. And though I struggled against Jade and Danielle, I was no match for two people.

Then I heard adult voices, and Debbie came running towards us yelling that Mr Bamber and the instructors were on their way. As soon as they heard that, Jade and Danielle fled into the woods, abandoning Bella and leaving me battered and bruised, but just about able to stand up. I hadn't noticed Our Angela following closely behind Debbie.

"Hold on, Louise," she shouted, "Gregor and Mr Bamber have gone to get some equipment." Then Angela saw me and her face went white.

"Don't worry about me, Angela," I said hoarsely. "Get Louise down before Bella knocks her down." Angela looked over and saw Bella inching closer to the sobbing Louise. She looked unsure what to do, but she didn't hesitate. I shouted to her not to look down and she didn't, just kept moving steadily upwards till she reached Louise. When Bella realised that Angela was on the scene, she quickly scrambled down. By this time Louise was weak and rooted to the rock. Angela tentatively climbed towards Louise and stretched out her hand till Louise could catch hold. This seemed to calm Louise down and Angela just kept talking though her own voice was weak with fear.

I don't know how Angela would have managed after that because Gregor, Cathy and Mr Bamber had all arrived kitted up and ready to help both Angela and Louise down to safety. Blankets were wrapped round Angela and Louise and they were escorted back to the Centre. Paramedics had also been summoned and the three of us were checked over to make sure that we were none the worse for our ordeal. I suffered minor cuts and bruises, but what was hurt most, I suppose, was my pride. I thought I was fit for Bella, but I wasn't as tough as I thought I was. I don't really mind, though, because I would never want to be like Bella – not in a million, trillion years. But, for the first time since we had left home, I wanted to phone and hear the familiar voices of Mum and Gran.

There was so much going on that I had forgotten about Bella and the two runaways, Jade and Danielle. I didn't even see them at mealtime in the restaurant where we tucked into pizzas and burgers and French fries. We went as planned into the recreation area, but before we started to play music or watch television, Mr Bamber gathered us round and said he had something to tell us. He looked very solemn, even in his casual clothes, but we listened as attentively as though he was taking an assembly back at school.

"Boys and girls, I don't wish to dwell too much on the events of the day, but I think you should know that a very serious incident has been averted and it is down to the quick thinking and courage of two people – Miss Winters and her young sibling, Samantha – I mean *Sam.* An accident has been averted, but the three culprits – I think you all know who they are – will be escorted back to Coatbridge in a police car, where they will be met by their parents. We also discovered some items in their room which may belong to some of you, and which I am sure you will be happy to have returned. It only remains for me to wish you an enjoyable evening and I think – and hope – that the remainder of our weekend will pass without incident."

He didn't sniff once during that long speech, but he did ask for a round of applause for Angela and me, and the cheers which followed almost knocked the roof off. And he was true to his word about the treats – up to the minute DVDs, crisps, cans of fizzy drinks and all the sweets we could eat. The rest of the evening was fun and friendly and free of Bella and her cronies who would be spending a much less pleasant evening at the police station waiting for their parents.

# Chapter 18

## My Teacher's My Sister!

I was exhausted and still smarting from my cuts and bruises when I went up to bed. I saw that Angela's door was ajar. She was sitting on the bed in her fluffy pyjamas (Yes, even my grown up sister still gets them from Gran at Christmas) combing out her wet hair. She looked drawn and exhausted.

It suddenly dawned on me that if Angela hadn't been my sister, I would probably have thought she was the most brilliant teacher in the world. Because that's what she is! As clear as the water flowing from the gorge waterfall, I could now see that things have to change; it's part of life. Just as the old school building has to go to make way for the new Summerlee Primary, Mrs McNulty had to move on and make way for the new generation of teachers like Our Angela. I could look ahead and see that Angela will probably grow old with the new building and know the generations of pupils as well as Mrs McNulty did.

I never once stopped to think of how Angela was feeling, how difficult it was for her in her very first teaching post. I could have made it so much easier for her, but I was so busy thinking of myself. What a first class twit!

I tiptoed into the room wanting to say something but the words just wouldn't come out. Angela turned round and stopped combing her hair. She didn't speak either. She just beamed an Angela smile at me – like the old days when she was just my sister – not my teacher. I couldn't help myself – I just threw my arms around her and gave her the most enormous hug and whispered, "You're the best sister *and* teacher in the world!"

For someone who is allergic to hugs – this is becoming a habit with me!

# Chapter 19

## Triple Trouble at Summerlee Heritage Park

You could be forgiven for thinking that my story is over. I've realised that my sister is a *great* teacher and a *fabulous* sister. She can go off and get married to Rob, I can go off to high school and we could 'all live happily ever after'. But, you would be forgetting that this is life and not a fairy tale – and the school session doesn't finish until June.

After our eventful weekend trip to Auchterallan Outdoor Centre, life at school returned to normal. Better than normal actually, because Bella, Jade and Danielle had been transferred to another school. It is difficult to put into words how the atmosphere in our class had changed. There was no tension, no animosity; we just got on with our work and the weeks rolled by pleasantly till we reached the Easter break at the beginning of April.

Angela and Rob were busy each day with plans for the wedding, but apart from one shopping trip to have a fitting for my bridesmaid's dress and to choose shoes and something for my hair, it was pretty much a relaxing holiday spent with my friends. We passed most of our days down at Summerlee Heritage Park, which is just a stone's throw from where we live.

There was a lot to see and do inside *Scotland's Noisiest Museum*. The Curator, Angus McPhee, was always telling us, "This, boys and girls, is HISTORY IN ACTION. See how your grandfathers and g-r-e-a-t grandfathers toiled in the mines and engineering workshops, so that you could live a life of l-u-x-u-r-y." (Mr McPhee had a strange way of making words stretch like elastic.)

But he was right. As soon as you walk through the heavy wrought iron gates, it's like stepping back into the past. To the right is a row of red brick buildings which house the Shop, an Exhibition Room and most importantly – the Cafe. In the distance stands a humongous hall made of red brick and corrugated iron, with a huge wall of windows at the far end which overlook the Railway Station and the Town Centre.

On the left is the Tram Terminus and tram line, which goes along past the Exhibition Hall, winding down towards the coal mine and row of miners' cottages. Behind the buildings, down a steep embankment is the canal – or what's left of it. On the bank of the canal are the excavations of the original Gartsherrie Iron Works. (The first time we visited the Heritage Park, we all thought that these were *Roman ruins*.)

The other thing I love about the Heritage Park is the fact that, as Mr McPhee is always quick to point out, "This is a *hands-on* museum." Imagine being encouraged to touch things and see how they work, instead of being told to 'keep our grubby hands off'. Then there were the special events at various points throughout the year, such as Steam Fairs and Fun Days with face painting, tram rides and market stalls.

And, this was one of the few places where I hadn't been in trouble or got into any 'scrapes', as my gran called them. One of her other sayings is that 'when trouble does come your way, it usually arrives in threes.'

Because it was the Easter Holidays, there was a special Easter Fair which lasted for a whole week. As well as the usual exhibitions and tram rides, we could try our hand at egg painting, face painting, rolling eggs and funfair rides too. Holly and I went there most days and usually bumped into people we knew from school or our neighbourhood. But, my first scrape that holiday actually involved my gran and a very rickety wheelchair.

One of the special events organised for the first week of the holidays was an exhibition entitled *A Trip Down Memory Lane.* Mum thought it would be a good idea to take Gran because she would recognise a lot of the stuff which was on display. We packed a picnic lunch and set off early because it was a sunny day and we wanted to make the most of the unusually good spell of weather after we had been into the Exhibition Hall and visited the row of old cottages. It was just me, Mum and Gran and the wheelchair which Gran hated, but which was necessary because the Heritage Park was so huge.

It all started off very well, with Mum pushing the chair and me carrying the picnic hamper. Our first stop was the replica of the old Co-op, where everyone shopped in Gran's day. "No big impersonal superstores in those days," she recalled, "just good quality products, personal service and you always had your *dividend* to look forward to." (Apparently that was the olden days' equivalent of *loyalty cards.)*

The shop was very small, cramped and dark, but Gran was in her element, recognising most of the products which were on the shelves and remembering the prices as well since – as she loved to remind us – she had worked in the Co-op till she got married and had her family. I particularly liked the heavy, old-fashioned cash register, even if it didn't scan the products or work by electricity. "No, dear," said Gran, "shop assistants knew the prices by heart *and* if there was a power cut, we could still use our tills and serve the customers."

Gran said a lot more on the subject of shops and shop assistants in her day, but I was itching to get back outside and into the sunshine. I was also feeling a bit peckish and hoping we would soon be stopping for a mid-morning snack.

We did eventually go outside, but Mum was enthralled by the sight of old fashioned games being demonstrated to a bunch of kids just outside the big Hall. There was a dressing up box with nurses' outfits and cowboy hats and an even bigger box with skipping ropes, yoyos, telephones and spinning tops – all of which reminded Mum of Christmases and birthdays past. I had put the picnic basket on Gran's lap and started pushing the wheelchair towards the picnic park down by the canal, hoping that this would spur Mum on to leave the games and follow us. Gran was quite chirpy and chattered on about the olden days, inspired by all of the things she had so far encountered during our visit. I was trying to keep my eye on the precarious picnic basket and look out for Mum's arrival while at the same time negotiating the movement of the wheelchair. So engrossed was I in my multi-tasking that I failed to notice a young boy on a skateboard whizzing towards us.

Before I knew it, I was swerving to avoid collision with the skateboard, lost control of the wheelchair which went hurtling down the steep path towards the canal, with Gran clutching the picnic basket with one hand while clasping one arm of the chair with the other and hollering, "Save me, someone pleeeeeeease!" I was puffing and panting after her, with Mum in hot pursuit shouting, "She's my mother! Help her! Help her!"

It is amazing the amount of stuff which flashes through your mind during split seconds of danger. I saw vivid newspaper headlines such as "GRAN DROWNED IN CANAL WITH PICNIC HAMPER" and "PENSIONER DIVES INTO CANAL AFTER WHEELCHAIR". Luckily for Gran and us, she was saved before the wheelchair reached the canal bank. Two park keepers were at the bottom of the hill and managed to jump onto the path and stop the runaway wheelchair before it could deposit Gran or the picnic lunch into the murky waters of the canal. Mum and I were both sobbing hysterically as we reached Gran who, by this time, was as cool as a cucumber and ready to comfort us as though *we* were the ones who had been in danger. The two heroic workmen pushed the wheelchair back up the path to safety, and checked the brakes and wheels to make sure that there was no damage done.

There was, in fact, a local newspaper headline which read, "GRITTY GRAN SAVED BY WORKERS IN CANAL DRAMA". Gran became a local celebrity after that and was told to visit the Heritage Park anytime as an *honoured guest.* I was later given a row by Mum for being careless and not paying attention to what I was doing. Nothing about her own carelessness in watching games when she should have been watching Gran! After all, I am strictly speaking still a *child!* (Of course, I didn't say these things out loud – then Mum would have added 'downright cheek' to my fast growing list of misdemeanours.)

***

My favourite event at the Heritage Park was *Storytelling Day*. I had been coming to this event for years and had come to recognise the band of storytellers and their stories. The storytellers were dotted around the park, adapting their tales to suit the surroundings. Whilst on the tram, Bert, a crusty old tram driver turned storyteller, would make up stories of magical tram journeys which spirited us away from Summerlee into far off lands and along mystical tram tracks. It was a bit like *Harry Potter Meets Dr. Who* sometimes, but Bert had such a wonderful, deep voice that he could have read out the telephone directory and made it sound exciting.

The row of miners' cottages also housed some storytellers. Since each cottage represented a different period in history, the stories were tailored to suit the period and mainly focused on the families' lives and the hardships they suffered. My favourite cottage was the one which depicted life in Victorian times, because I liked that period of history in class. I would listen to the tales of young children being sent down the mines and into factories and mills when they should have been in school. I think Gran would have been great in one of the cottages telling her stories about growing up during the Second World War. She says she doesn't mind telling us, but she didn't fancy the public knowing 'her business'.

I usually saved the coalmine to the last, because it was dark and damp and full of atmosphere and this is where my second scrape occurred. I was with Holly and the Twins and Paul and Andrew. Now, when the two boys were with us, things tended to be more mischievous. Their attention span, when it wasn't focusing on football, was virtually zero, and cries of "We're bored!" filled the air. The storyteller in the coalmine was called Lizzie and she was a first year drama student who was doing storytelling as part of her course.

Lizzie seemed very nervous as this was her first story in the mine. It also turned out that she was scared of the dark and was trying to overcome her fear at the same time. (It wasn't pitch dark since we were all expected to wear miners' helmets complete with torch lights on the brim, though they did cast an eerie glow in the cave-like coal mine.) Her story was about a young boy, Billy, who was forced down the mine and suffered cruelly at the hands of a wicked foreman called Bresslaw. The mine was packed – well, the numbers were limited to twenty – as Lizzie started her story. We were behind Lizzie, beside a tableau of children loading coal into huge baskets. Lizzie was stumbling over her words and just couldn't seem to get her confidence going. Paul had the bright idea that we should help her out by livening up the story. He and Andrew started making ghostly sounds, very quiet at first, then gradually getting louder. Debbie and Louise didn't realise that the noises *weren't* ghosts, so they started whimpering in unison, spreading panic around the cramped mine.

By this time, some of the younger children were getting scared and tugging at their parents to take them out. Poor Lizzie was trying to keep her story going whilst looking round frantically to detect where the noises were coming from. In my haste to put my hand over Paul's mouth to quieten him, I bumped against one of the dummies which fell forward onto one of the baskets which then emptied its load of fake coal all over Lizzie. Poor Lizzie yelled like the banshees we had read about in old Scottish tales and legends. (If there is a test at her drama college for screaming, she will certainly pass with flying colours!) There was a mass exit, with parents, children and Lizzie abandoning the mine as though escaping from some kind of explosion.

We stayed in the mine, afraid to show our faces until the coast was clear. "I was only trying to help Lizzie," Paul whispered, though there was little chance of anyone hearing him above the commotion which was happening outside the mine.

"I know you were," said Holly, also in hushed tones, while the Twins still sobbed uncontrollably.

"It was definitely a ghost!" they cried in that spooky way they have of uttering their words at exactly the same second.

"It wasn't a ghost," I said sharply. "It was me trying to hush Paul and stop him from scaring Lizzie. I'm to blame for this whole mess."

"We were all enjoying the frightened reactions of the crowd, Sam, so we are all to blame," Andrew said trying to make me feel better and the others agreed.

The noise outside the mine seemed to have died down, so we plucked up courage to go outside and, as my Gran would say, 'face the music'. We had to return our helmets to a little hut just outside the mine. A tearful Lizzie was inside hugging a cup of steaming tea and being comforted by Ellen, one of the Heritage Park volunteers, a sprightly pensioner who had a hearty laugh.

"Here comes trouble," she said as we entered, not realising that the Twins might take her literally and confess to their part in the *crime in the coalmine*. I had no intention of avoiding responsibility, but the Twins made it sound worse than it really was. I could just see Mum's face when I told her we had been banned from the Heritage Park for life and Gran would be unable to make the most of her honorary status because of the shame.

But, when we explained how it was a joke that had backfired, and how we thought we could help Lizzie, Ellen just did that hearty laugh thing which was so infectious that we all joined in – even Lizzie, who joked that we would all probably graduate from drama school before she did.

*** 

There was more than one crisp, sunny day during that holiday and my two near disasters hadn't put me off visiting Summerlee Heritage Park. Holly and I were just coming out of the Cafe one afternoon, when we met the Twins and Andrew and Paul, who were just boarding the tram. They called out to us to join them. Luckily, we had already purchased our tickets from the shop, so we were able to climb on after them, just as the tram was about to leave. It wasn't a very long trip, about fifteen minutes doing a circular route of the Park, making two stops – one at the mines and one at the cottages before returning to the main gates.

We were so engrossed in chatting that we didn't notice the new additions to the passengers when we stopped at the mines. But, when Holly and I stood up to get off and visit the old cottages, we found our way blocked.

It was Bella, flanked as usual by Jade and Danielle.

"I thought there was a funny smell when we got on this bus. Isn't that right, girls?" said Bella, directing her comments to the two girls behind her in the narrow aisle, but keeping her gaze fixed on me. I was shocked to see her. I hadn't given her a thought for weeks. I assumed that she would have moved to another town as well as school, but that was wishful thinking. There were several other primary schools in Coatbridge which Bella hadn't tried and which didn't involve moving house.

Most of the passengers had already gone off the tram, and Mr McPhee had stepped down to let people show their tickets. It was just us and Bella and she was spoiling for a fight. (No change there.) I finally found my voice and my confidence.

"If there's a smell on this tram, Bella, you and your pals brought it on with you. Now, shift yourselves so that I can get off and breathe in some fresh air." The determination in my voice didn't match what I was feeling inside. Bella hesitated for a moment, stared straight at me clenching her fists as though ready to throw a punch. My palms were sweating, but I knew that if she tried anything, I wouldn't let her get away with it. I knew a fight with Bella in a place like this would be very public, and this time I *would* be banned. I hoped that Bella didn't do mind reading. Suddenly, Bella moved aside to let us pass. I moved as casually as I could, making my way along the aisle and back into the sunshine. Andrew and Paul had followed us too. I don't think they were scared of Bella, but simply wanted to see if I was all right.

Once off the tram, Mr McPhee asked us if there had been any trouble, but we said "No," that we had just met someone we used to know from school. As the tram was about to set off along the track, Bella pulled down the window and leaned out.

"Don't think I've forgotten about Auchterallan. I'll get even with you and your snotty sister. You just wait and see!" she shouted as the tram chugged off into the distance.

"Don't worry about Bella," said Paul, "she's all talk."

I wanted to believe that. I really did. But something inside made me think that we hadn't seen or heard the last of Bully Bella.

\*\*\*

I managed to put our encounter with Bella to the back of my mind and enjoy the remainder of the Easter Holidays. Dad was at home for Easter Sunday and Monday, which was good for the whole family. Even Mum had time off from her business because most of her clients had their hair and beauty treatments before Easter. The sun continued to shine while we, as a family, just chilled out and chatted till before we knew it, Angela and I were back at school, Mum and Dad were back at work and Gran was back to baking and *Countdown*.

# Chapter 20

# Miss Greenfingers and the Eco Enemies

If we thought that this final term before going to high school was going to be a relaxing one, we were soon put right when Angela outlined the activities which needed to be completed before the school could be presented with its Eco Flag. Poor Angela – I don't know where she got her energy and enthusiasm from: not only was she planning a wedding and putting us through our final P7 paces, but she had managed to write a short play which our class would rehearse and perform on the day of the Eco Presentation. *Ms Snobby* had tried to put her off, suggesting that we could perform a musical item instead, which would involve less preparation. I overheard Angela saying to Rob, "I think she's jealous, Rob. I don't know why. She's promoted and will probably be a Head Teacher before long. I just can't seem to do anything right as far as she's concerned."

Of course, Angela would never speak to me about *Ms Snobby* in that way. She was too professional. But, I think *Ms Snobby is* jealous of Our Angela. Mr Bamber 'sang her praises' (Gran again) during a school assembly when we returned from Auchterallan. (He praised me as well.) I could see that *Ms Snobby's* blotches were out in force, probably because she was jealous of how well Angela is coping. (You would think her blotches would have turned green in that case, wouldn't you?) How does a mere child like me arrive at such a conclusion? Well, I had been jealous of Angela too. Remember?

Our school days were spent in the Eco-garden, helping our Caretaker, Bill Watson who was responsible for preparing the ground to allow us to plant trees and flowers. Most of the boys in the class were keen to help out there because, in his youth, Bill had been a professional footballer, and had once played for the Coatbridge team, Albion Rovers. (Dad always jokes that there were more Albion Rovers' players on the pitch than there were supporters in the stand, but I would never say that to Bill.) We all looked up to him. He had been coaching our school football team for years and was responsible for many medals and trophies finding their way into the glass cabinets in the foyer of the school. Each class in the school was responsible for its own little patch, and now that the days were brighter and longer, a splash of colour was evident as the plants were peeping through the soil.

In class, posters and leaflets were being produced and inspected and displayed on walls in and around the school. Rotas were drawn up to collect litter and several pupils from our class were appointed Eco Monitors, whose job it was to patrol the school at intervals and lunchtimes making sure that pupils – and staff – were using the bins provided. We felt very grown up and important, and we seemed to take greater pride in the school and its appearance. Mr Bamber said that if these good habits were transferred to the new building, it would remain 'in mint condition for years to come'.

To add to our excitement, we were rehearsing our Eco Play every spare moment we could find. There was a part for everyone in the class – Angela was determined that no one should be left out. The play was called *The*

*Litter Louts and the Eco Gang* and as the title suggests, it dealt with the theme of responsibility for keeping public and private places free from litter and vandalism. Angela had chosen names which reflected each character's personality. The leader of the 'Litter Louts' was called 'Todd Trash' and his sidekick was called 'Vicky Vandal'. (I had volunteered to play the part of Vicky, though I knew who I would be basing her character on. In fact, I wondered if Our Angela hadn't been thinking of Bella when she wrote the part.) Members of their gang had names like 'Ricky Rubbish', 'Danny Dump', 'Gordon Graffiti' and 'Lucy Litterbug'.

The 'Eco Gang' had characters whose names were associated with keeping clean or tidy. Their leader was called 'Big Dom' and his sidekick was called 'Wheelie Bin'. Other members of the gang were called: 'Jif', 'Mophead', twins called 'Debbie Daz' and 'Lucy Lux' who were to be known as The Soapsud Sisters. (No prizes for guessing who would be playing those roles. I think they were thrilled that Angela had written twins into her play and it made them feel really special.)

The play was both funny and fun to do, but it also sent out a serious message – that it was 'cool to be clean' and that every individual was responsible for his or her own litter. We were also excited that we would be performing it in front of lots of important people as well as our relatives and friends. Dad said he would make sure he was home that week so that he wouldn't miss my star performance. Mum was really pleased when Angela asked her to help out with make-up and costumes because of her acting experience as well as her hair and beauty skills. Everything was going so well until two things happened in quick succession – and they both involved Bella.

It was the week of the play and – hopefully – the presentation of our Eco Flag. We stayed behind each evening after school to rehearse the play. Paul, who was playing Todd Trash, and I had come out into the yard to rehearse one of our scenes when we heard a commotion coming from the direction of the garden area. We thought it might be some of the cast larking about, but we went to investigate anyway. Luckily for us that we did. When we reached the garden, we saw Bella, Jade and Danielle whooping with delight as they stomped through our gardens, pulling up plants and throwing them over the wall. We knew that Bill Watson was in the Assembly Hall, so we did what we could to chase Bella and the others away. She didn't make a move until she saw me get out my mobile phone and start dialling. I didn't know the number for the police, but Bella wasn't taking any chances, as she vaulted the wall with ease, with her cronies clambering clumsily after her.

When Bill and Angela saw the mess, Bill contacted Mr Bamber, as well as informing the police. Here we were, rehearsing a play about vandalism and Bella was outside performing worse deeds than the Litter Louts. Bella could be dealt with later, but the mess she had left behind left us worrying how we could rectify it in time for the Eco Inspection which was only two days away. We didn't have the heart for any further rehearsal that evening, but we certainly knew what we would be doing the following day – cleaning up the real life Vicky Vandal's mess!

Fortunately, the fine weather continued and Bill Watson organised groups to tidy up the mess while he replanted some of the flowers which had been damaged. Everyone – staff *and* pupils – pulled together to make sure that the flower beds were as pretty as they had been before Bella had messed them up. We were a bit more upbeat by the time we had to carry on with rehearsals, and this setback had made us more determined that everything would go as planned. It was hard to pick ourselves up initially, because we had heard whispers that Bella hadn't been caught by the police. Yet again, nothing could be proved against her, but we couldn't let her spoil things, even when she wasn't part of our school any more.

But, we were on our guard. If Bella thought she had beaten us and escaped any kind of punishment, I felt sure she would come back to see what other damage she could inflict. I got together with Holly, the Twins and Andrew and Paul. We decided to have a rota during our evening rehearsals: two people to patrol the grounds when their scenes weren't being rehearsed. That way, if Bella did return, we could hopefully, catch her in the act.

We didn't have long to wait.

It was the evening before the Big Event and we were in the middle of our dress rehearsal. There was so much to do and we were running later than usual. It had started to get dark, making it more difficult to spot anything dodgy during our patrols. Holly and I had come out for a breath of fresh air; it was really stifling inside the hall because of the stage lights. We decided to test each other's lines and were becoming really caught up in our scene, when we heard the familiar voices of the Twins as they ran breathlessly towards us.

"There's someone over by the big wheelie bins," they hissed.

"It's probably a dog or a cat," suggested Holly, who was keen to return to our little rehearsal.

"No, I'm positive it's a person – in fact *more* than one person," said Debbie urgently.

"Yes, we heard talking," said Louise, clutching her sister's arm, as though the *voices* might come to get her.

"Let's check it out just in case. I wouldn't put it past Bella to revisit the scene of her crime," I said. I sent the Twins to fetch the school caretaker, Bill Watson, just in case it was someone other than Bella. Holly and I made our way quietly to the bin sheds which stood right next to the main building.

We saw the flames before we saw Bella. She was standing holding on to a petrol can, admiring her 'handiwork'. Each time the flames shot higher, she laughed like a hyena and urged Jade and Danielle to do the same. I was scared. This was the worst damage Bella had ever inflicted. What's more, the wheelie bins were set against the school wall, and the sparks and flames were getting closer to the roof. Holly and I stayed out of Bella's sight and earshot. We didn't want to alert her, but we were afraid of the damage which was being caused to our school.

Then it dawned on me – the wall against which the wheelie bins were standing was the wall of the Assembly Hall where Angela was rehearsing the play. I had to act quickly. I whispered to Holly to get Bill Watson to call the Fire Service and get Angela to evacuate the building, while I would try to keep Bella talking so that she couldn't escape. Easier said than done. If Bella had been on her own, I might be successful, but as my experience at Auchterallan proved, I was no match for Bella *and* her two obedient pals.

I stepped forward, shaking like a leaf inside, but trying to speak without stammering.

"Caught in the act, Bella! You won't be able to escape this time."

Bella looked startled for a second, and then she found her voice, which was rather hoarse from screeching. "Look what's crawled out of the woodwork, girls. A louse!" and she cackled at her own joke.

Neither Danielle nor Jade made any reply, but they did smile half-heartedly. In fact, it occurred to me that they rarely spoke, just listened to Bella and nodded their approval. They were kept around as admirers, not really Bella's equals or friends. I could have felt sorry for them at that moment, if the situation hadn't been so dangerous. I was wishing that some adult would turn up soon because I wasn't really sure what to do next. It always seemed so easy in books, or films, or even plays. Perhaps I needed to put on my Vicky Vandal persona and speak to Bella in language she would surely understand. Or better still, speak to Jade and Danielle and persuade them that sticking around with Bella will only get them into serious trouble. It was worth a try.

"Jade and Danielle, are you going to let Bella ruin your lives as well as her own?" I said in my toughest Vicky Vandal voice. "She's not really your pal. All you two are to her is her alibi. Think about it." I hoped they wouldn't think about it for too long, because the flames were edging closer to the roof and a thick, black smoke was now swirling about and catching my throat. But it didn't really matter, because I heard voices and the warning sound of the approaching fire engine.

As soon as Bella realised she was about to be caught, she dropped the can and made a run for it. I wasn't going to let her disappear so easily. I jumped forward and caught hold of her hair, swung her round and round so that she became dizzy. All the while she was screaming at Jade and Danielle to get me off her. Jade and Danielle, however, made their own attempt to escape, but tripped each other up in their confusion and ended up in a heap. Bella had managed to break free and headed away from the fire and towards the high brick wall which surrounded the school building. Bella started climbing, and we all knew how good she was at that. Bill Watson, who had been out walking his little Scotch terrier when he was alerted to the fire, came running towards us, still clutching Gizmo's lead. In the excitement, the dog broke loose and stood at the bottom of the wall barking up at Bella.

What happened next is more astonishing than the events of the whole evening. That tiny little dog jumped up, managing to sink his teeth into Bella's ankle and she let out such a yell of pure terror. Unable to free herself and continue her escape, Bella turned into a gibbering wreck.

"Get this monster away from me! Get it off! I'm terrified of dogs!"

Bella – who had terrorised the whole school for years – was a scaredy cat when it came to dogs. She was terrified of a *terrier*! It's a pity that our caretaker had only made a present of this dog to his wife recently. In the midst of all this drama, while the fire fighters were doing what they do best – putting out the wheelie bin fire – we burst out laughing. Bella looked so comical with Gizmo's little teeth embedded in the hem of her jeans. What's more, when the police arrived, she practically begged to be taken down to the station – minus Gizmo, of course.

What a night! What excitement! What relief! And what a *mess* to be cleared up before our important visitors arrived at the school! At least, there would still be a school for them to see when they did come, and not a burnt out shell.

# Chapter 21

# The Unfair Records' Fair and the Almost Unhappy Ending

We did manage to clear up the mess left by the fire. We did put on our Eco Play. We did get our Eco Flag. The month of May had started and ended with sunshine which continued right into June – our last month of Primary School and the final month *ever* for Summerlee Primary – *as we knew it.*

What can I say except that it was HECTIC! More preparations, this time for our Graduation Ceremony. More practising of songs and speeches. More class collections – this time to buy a wedding gift for Angela and Rob. Gran went on line to look at Angela's Wedding List (said 'it wasn't like that in my day; we got what people chose as gifts and were perfectly content'*)* and ordered a crystal bowl which could be used as a centrepiece to hold fruit or pot pourri. She even wrapped it up for us and we had real bother keeping it hidden from Angela until Graduation Day and our final Assembly ...

But, before we got to that most eventful day, my nosiness almost resulted in an unhappy-ever-after scenario which would have put all of my other mishaps in the shade.

Our garage has never been used for its original purpose – to protect our two cars from car thieves and the frequent rainy weather we seem to have in Coatbridge. In fact, I don't think anyone in our street actually puts their cars *inside* the garages, preferring instead to crowd the driveways or take up valuable pavement space. My dad has converted our garage into a 'Music Room' where he stores his vast record collection and D.J. equipment. He was once a Disc Jockey (D.J.), which is apparently someone who plays 'records' at night clubs or 'Discos' as they were referred to in his 'young' days. (He even shortened his name, Arthur, to 'Art' to make it more 'cool'.)

"I don't know why you want to hold onto those old records, Arthur, when these days it's all MP3 Players and modern gadgets which download music – and take up much less space," my mum keeps saying in the hope that one day he'll take her advice, if only to stop her nagging.

Dad always looks really hurt when anyone mentions getting rid of his beloved collection of 'vintage vinyl'. "These records will be collectors' items one day," he says huffily, "worth a fortune, they are."

"If that's the case, why don't you sell them on E-Bay and use the money to convert the garage into a sitting-room for your mother?" says my mum thinking that the best way to a husband's heart is by making him feel guilty about his own mother.

Mum was always quick to spot an opportunity to get rid of the records *and* find more space for Grandma Winters, who has been living in our tiny box room since Grandpa died a few years back.

You are by now, fully aware of the importance of my gran to our household and how we could never imagine our lives without her. Therefore, you will also understand my predicament when I heard the tail end of a telephone conversation between my Gran and my dad who was away on one of his *Old Dears' Tours* to the Lake District.

"Arthur, you know how I hate being in the way ... it's about time I got out from under Sandra's feet. I'll get ready to move my stuff ... "

My heart sank – my gran was talking about leaving – and it sounded like a permanent move! I didn't want to hear anymore. Why had no-one told me? It was like the Angela saga all over again. I went to my room to think. I had to come up with a plan to make Gran stay – and I had to come up with it soon, because wherever Gran was going, it sounded as though she would be going sooner rather than later.

I didn't have long to wait for a suitable idea. Summerlee Heritage Park had a huge advert on a billboard beside the entrance – *Bumper Records' Fair*. I could, as Gran might say, 'kill two birds with one stone' – clear the garage of Dad's musty old record collection, make way for Gran's new room and pay for it with the proceeds of the sale of the records. (Would that be *three* birds then?) Dad never played them anyway, so he would be pleased; Mum would be glad to be rid of them because she was always moaning about them; and Gran would surely be 'over the moon' that she didn't have to move out after all.

There was only one snag – I only had a few days to empty the garage *and I* had to find a way to transport the records to the Heritage Park without anyone noticing. I wanted it to be a big surprise.

Luckily for me I have the best friends in the world who were willing to help me carry out this magnificent plan. Holly, the Twins, Andrew and Paul came over with baskets and boxes and trolleys and trailers and we set to work. They had heard about Dad's record collection but they hadn't seen it before; in fact they weren't really sure what a *record* was. Mr McPhee, the Caretaker at Summerlee Heritage Park, had arranged to open the gates early on the Saturday morning to allow us to transport Dad's record collection to the Exhibition Hall where the Fair was being held. He also provided us with a table to display the records – free of charge, because I had told him the money was for my gran's new room. (Remember, my gran is an honorary guest at the Heritage Park after the almost-disaster at the canal.)

Don't imagine it was easy to transport zillions of records without drawing attention to ourselves. When I opened the garage door to reveal wall to wall records, *singles, EPs and LPs*, my friends were gobsmacked.

"Wow, it's like Aladdin's Cave," said Holly.

"I just wish we could rub Aladdin's lamp and transport this stuff to the Heritage Park," said Andrew looking from the boxes of records to the small basket on the front of his bicycle. He picked up an LP by a band called *The Beatles*.

"Look at the size of this," he said. "It looks gigantic compared to a CD. And it's *so* heavy."

"How did your dad manage to play these in the car?" asked Debbie.

"Well these things are made of vinyl," I explained feeling quite important about my superior knowledge of prehistoric music. "They were only meant to be played on something called a 'record player' which had to stay in the one room."

"Give me an *iPod* any day," said Paul.

Holly, the organised one of our group, reminded us of the need to get a move on or we would be caught, or miss the Fair, or both. Luckily for me, Saturday was Gran's baking day and she was busy in the kitchen which was at the back of our house. I made sure she didn't become suspicious by popping in every so often to try out the goodies. It's a wonder she didn't notice that each time I came into the kitchen, I looked more bedraggled and somewhat out of breath. But, when Gran is in the baking zone, she is oblivious to everything and everyone around her.

Without the help of a magic genie, but with the assistance of my friends, we just managed to get our stall set up minutes before the opening. We were gobsmacked at how busy the place was and how popular these relics of the music world seemed to be. At first, we weren't sure what to charge, but Andrew and Paul checked out the other stalls to get an idea of prices. It was difficult to keep pace with the number of buyers who came and went from our stall, but they never left empty-handed. At one point, we were so busy that Mr McPhee stepped in to help us. I felt that Dad would have been so proud of how popular his collection was and proud of us for being such good salespersons. Andrew and Paul excelled, and the Twins with their sweet smiles made the customers feel they were getting the best bargains. Holly took charge of the mountains of coins we had accumulated, making sure that they were stored safely until the fair had ended.

In actual fact, our stall was sold out well before the end of the day, and before most of the other stalls. We were exhausted, but excited at the thoughts that we had earned enough money to create a new luxurious living space for Gran. Dad would be home that very evening and we would have time to count the money and present it to him.

In fact, we were still upstairs in my room counting the last few coins when I heard Dad's car turn into the drive way. We had been careful to put the coins into the little plastic bags provided by banks. (Mum has an endless supply for her business.) Holly had carefully counted all of the notes and added them to her tally of the coins. We felt like millionaires who had just completed a successful business deal. We had just packed the last of the money into a carrier bag when we heard the loud wail, like an animal in pain. We rushed downstairs thinking perhaps that there had been some kind of accident in the kitchen. I noticed that the front door was lying wide open and could hear the frantic voices of Mum and Gran. I was afraid to go outside ...

Dad had opened the garage door and was staring inside as though he had come upon a ghost. His face was as white as one of Gran's laundered tablecloths, and he was staring into the black space that was the garage. He was clutching something in his hand and muttering over and over: "We've been robbed ... we've been robbed ... been robbed ... robbed ..."

"Someone's been into the garage and stolen your dad's whole record collection," said Mum, not looking as happy as I thought she would to see that the records had gone. In fact, there were tears in her eyes and they weren't tears of joy. Dad, like a zombie, took an LP from the carrier bag in his hand and stared mournfully at it and then at the empty Aladdin's Cave where his records had been stored.

"Look, Sandra," he said in the saddest voice I have ever heard, "I finally found the missing Beatles' album for my collection – *Please, Please Me* – and now there's no collection to put it with."

"You'd better get onto the police straight away," said Gran. "The thieves can't have gotten very far with all the records you have collected over the years."

"You don't have to call the police," I blurted out before anyone could reach the phone. "I know what has happened to the records and I think you will be *pleased*, Dad, when I tell you."

You know, I really believed they would all be jumping for joy when I told them about the *Records' Fair* and the money we had raised to renovate the garage for Gran. I really did. But, as you well know, there is no pleasing adults sometimes. I told them about the phone call and Gran's plans to move out. I told them that I had cleared the garage *with a little help from my friends.* (Would you believe that is the title of a song by those *Beatles* Dad is so fond of?) Holly and the others handed over the bags of money – so we waited and waited ...

They laughed. First of all, it was a titter from Gran, then a snigger from Mum, then Dad looked at his one, solitary LP, then the money and then let out such a loud guffaw that I thought he was going to burst. All of that work and planning and lifting and transporting and selling and counting – and it was all one big joke to them while my friends and I just stood like confused statues and waited for an explanation.

My dad tried to talk in between hysterical bouts of laughter. "You sold thousands of pounds worth of vintage vinyl because – I can't believe I am saying this – because you thought your gran was leaving home and – and you were going to pay for the renovations with how much?"

"£532.63p, Mr Winters," said Holly in a matter-of-fact tone which seemed out of place with the rest of the madness. "We sold out in a matter of hours."

The Twins piped up together, "Yes, Mr McPhee, the Caretaker, said it was a *record* amount!" My dad was about to say something in reply, but thought better of it and just turned to Gran and said, "Tell her, Mum. Tell Sam what we *really* discussed regarding your *move.*"

Gran came and put her arms round me, "You see, Sam dear, your father was telling me that there was no need for me to 'get out from under your mother's feet' by taking a holiday because after the wedding he would be fixing up Angela's room as a sitting-room where I could have, as you young people say, *my own space.*"

I could feel the tears welling up in my eyes. "You mean," I blubbered, "there was no need to empty the garage? There was no need to get rid of Dad's record collection?"

Now I was in bits, and Holly and the Twins sobbed in sympathy while Andrew and Paul blushed with embarrassment – though I'm not exactly sure whether it was because of our tears or the humongous mistake I had involved them in. Trust Gran to save the day. "Right, everyone, inside for tea, cakes and bags of sympathy. And that's an order!"

Dad sat for the rest of the evening in shock, clutching his one and only LP. Once my friends had gone home, I went to my room. I didn't want to look at Dad's sad face and think about how I had ruined his hobby and cost him lots of money which would take me a lifetime of pocket money to repay. My dad doesn't bear grudges, so he did speak to me before he went off on his next trip. He told me that I acted the way I did out of kindness, though I had let him, Mum and Gran down by being so secretive. He admitted that it was irresponsible of him to keep a valuable record collection in a garage, so we both had lessons to learn.

I offered to place an advert in the newspaper to track down his collection, but he said that he would use the money to buy an *iPod* (Gran's suggestion, not mine) and I could download the music he had lost onto it. (Imagine being able to download all of that ancient stuff, though I didn't say this to Dad.) He said it would be much more useful and entertaining to listen to the music while he was away from home. He also said it would drown out the moans and groans of some of the *Old Dears* on his tours – but I must on no account tell Gran that he had said that.

# Chapter 21

## Speeches and Sniffles

We didn't have much time to dwell on that incident because the next few weeks flew by and before we knew it, the last day of our P7 had arrived.

Summerlee Primary School Hall was packed with proud parents, guardians, grandparents, aunties, uncles and, of course – the pupils. We were all pristine in our school uniforms, which perhaps were rather tighter and shorter after almost a year of growing. We had hired special Graduation Gowns and were to be presented with ties for our new high school as a parting gift. As I gazed at the stage decked with flowers, staff chatting and smiling and waiting for the Head Teacher to enter with the invited guests before the ceremony could get under way, I couldn't help thinking of that other Assembly last August, when I first learned that my Big Sister was going to be my teacher. I looked at her now, smiling down at me – only this time I smiled back and gave a little sisterly wave.

I could just see Mum and Dad and Gran, who was sporting a ruby red walking-stick to match her outfit. Mum was looking very glamorous too, wearing one of the *five* outfits she had bought for Angela's wedding. Every time she went to the shops, she had seen something which she thought was *definitely a sensational Mother-of-the-Bride outfit.* It was great to be sitting beside my friends, knowing there was no Bella to spoil our special occasion. I didn't mind sitting through another of Mr Bamber's long-winded speeches, I didn't mind waiting ages to receive my new tie. I just wanted the occasion to go on and on.

Towards the end of the ceremony, I had been given permission to present our class wedding gift and a bunch of flowers to Angela. I had asked Dennis Grant to present the flowers; I had never quite forgiven myself for the spider incident, even if he had. We walked forward nervously towards Angela who was beaming with pride and happiness. Suddenly, something strange came over me. I saw the microphone and I just made my way towards it and started speaking.

"Ladies and Gentlemen – and Mr Bamber, I would just like to say on behalf of Primary Seven, how much we are going to miss Summerlee Primary and – Miss Winters, *the best teacher in the whole world*!" That got a huge cheer and the pupils stomping their feet on the wooden floor. When the noise died down, I continued, "I'm going to be busy this summer. You see, I'm going to be bridesmaid at my big sister's wedding, but I promise to leave the wedding photos in the album and not on my phone."

Everyone laughed at that – even *Ms Snobby* managed a smile.

# Chapter 22

## And finally...

It has taken me a whole year – well *a whole school year* to realise how lucky I am!

My gran is the best cook in the world. My dad is the best coach driver in the world. My mother might have been a famous Diva if she had started her career early and not become the best wife and mother in the world. My sister is a BRILLIANT teacher who will no doubt be a Head Teacher one day to add to her honour of being Head Girl; in fact she will probably manage to be a brilliant wife, mum and teacher all at the same time!

I'm off to High School, my first day at the BIG SCHOOL as Gran calls it. No Little Pony lunch box or Mum holding my hand. No big sister waltzing in announcing she's my teacher. Probably a bigger number of Bully Bellas, but I'll just set Gizmo on them. Nope. I'm going to keep my head down and my nose clean. Who knows, I may even become Head Girl or at the very least, Captain of the Girls' Football Team. I hear they're very good ...